HIDE BEHIND THE MOON

Books by Beverly Lewis

GIRLS ONLY (GO!)
Youth Fiction

Dreams on Ice
Only the Best
A Perfect Match
Reach for the Stars
Follow the Dream
Better Than Best
Photo Perfect
Star Status

SUMMERHILL SECRETS
Youth Fiction

Whispers Down the Lane
Secret in the Willows
Catch a Falling Star
Night of the Fireflies
A Cry in the Dark
House of Secrets
Echoes in the Wind
Hide Behind the Moon
Windows on the Hill
Shadows Beyond the Gate

HOLLY'S HEART
Youth Fiction

Best Friend, Worst Enemy
Secret Summer Dreams
Sealed With a Kiss
The Trouble With Weddings
California Crazy
Second-Best Friend
Good-Bye, Dressel Hills
Straight-A Teacher
No Guys Pact
Little White Lies
Freshman Frenzy
Mystery Letters

www.BeverlyLewis.com

03B

HIDE BEHIND THE MOON

Beverly Lewis

BETHANY HOUSE PUBLISHERS
MINNEAPOLIS, MINNESOTA 55438

Hide Behind the Moon

Cover illustration by Chris Ellison

Published by Bethany House Publishers
11400 Hampshire Avenue South
Bloomington, Minnesota 55438
www.bethanyhouse.com

Bethany House Publishers is a Division of
Baker Book House Company, Grand Rapids, Michigan

Printed in the United States of America by
Bethany Press International, Bloomington, Minnesota 55438

Library of Congress Cataloging-in-Publication Data

Lewis, Beverly, 1949–
Hide behind the moon / by Beverly Lewis.
p. cm. — (SummerHill secrets ; 8)
Summary: Merry's Amish friend Rachel asks for help with her Runschpringa, the period in her teen years when she can experiment with the outside world and modern life before deciding to devote herself to Plain living.
ISBN 1-55661-874-3 (pbk.)
[1. Amish—Fiction. 2. Friendship—Fiction. 3. Christian life—Fiction.] I. Title. II. Series: Lewis, Beverly, 1949–
SummerHill secrets ; 8.
PZ7.L5846Hi 1998 97–45421
[Fic]—dc21 CIP
AC

For Larissa
with love.

BEVERLY LEWIS is a speaker, teacher, and the best-selling author of the HOLLY'S HEART series. She has written over forty books for adults, teens, and children. Many of her articles and stories have appeared in the nation's top magazines.

Beverly is a member of The National League of American Pen Women and the Society of Children's Book Writers and Illustrators. She and her husband, Dave, along with their three teenagers, live in Colorado. She fondly remembers their cockapoo named Cuddles, who used to snore to Mozart!

"There's all the difference in the world, you know, between being inside looking out and outside looking in."

—from *Anne of Windy Poplars*
by L.M. Montgomery

ONE

"Shh! We daresn't be heard," whispered Rachel Zook, my Amish girlfriend. Silently, she leaned over the old attic trunk and pulled open the heavy lid. Her eyes were filled with glee.

"I can't believe I let you talk me into this," I said, looking around at our creepy surroundings. "Cobwebs aren't exactly my cup of tea."

She stifled a giggle. "*Ach*, leave it to you, Merry Hanson. You ain't scared, now, are ya?"

The musty darkness stretched all the way under the attic eaves in both directions. Rachel's kerosene lantern swayed back and forth from the rafters, casting lively shadows over wooden crates and old canning jars.

"So *this* is what an Amish attic's supposed to look like," I teased. "Thought it'd be more organized."

"It's about as *ret* up as it can be. Besides, lookee here, I think I might've found somethin'." She stood up, brushing the dust off the sleeves of her purple dress and long black apron, staring at the dilapidated-looking stationery box in her hand.

I inched closer, very curious. "You sure it's such a

good idea to snoop like this?"

Rachel's blue eyes were serious, determined. "I'm getting warmer," she said. "I can feel it in my bones."

"Well, *I'm* cold. It's freezing up here." I waited for her to take the hint, but she kept rummaging through the box, searching for what, I didn't know exactly.

"I'm almost positive there're some old poems up here," she muttered to herself.

"Well, they can wait, right? Till summer, maybe?"

"But we're here now . . . and Dat and Mam are gone for a bit. *Jah*, I think we best go ahead and keep lookin'."

Rachel motioned for me to come over to help, so I did. After all, she was one of my dearest friends in all of Lancaster County. SummerHill, to be exact.

Oh, she'd gotten this hare-brained notion that there was a strain of writing talent in her family somewhere, and she just had to prove it to her "English" friend, namely me. *English* meaning I wasn't Amish. Or as Rachel, who was nearly sixteen, often said, "You're my English cousin."

Technically, I *was* related to her. My Swiss ancestors and Rachel's had arrived in America back in 1737 on the same boat—*The Charming Nancy*. We shared a common relative—Joseph Lapp, one of my great-great-grandfathers—which made us distant cousins.

"Here's another big box," I said, pulling it out of a hodgepodge of quilts and linens and things. "Looks like a diary."

"Let's have a look-see," she said.

I sat on another dusty trunk near the lantern's eerie

circle of light, observing as she opened the oblong wooden box.

She rummaged through some loose papers inside, but nothing seemed to catch her interest. "Nah, nothin' much here."

Growing impatient, I asked, "Isn't it about time to be making doughnuts again?" I wanted to get her mind off her present pursuit and start her contemplating the prospect of sweets, one of her weaknesses.

"Jah, this Saturday we'll be making some," she replied, still nosing around in the trunk.

"Well, am I invited?"

She stopped her searching, glancing over at me. "Of course you're invited. What'sa matter with ya, askin' something so foolish?"

I just smiled, watching her bend over and remove several more boxes from the bottomless trunk, or so it seemed.

"Better put everything back the way you found it," I told her.

"Ach, as if I ain't smart enough to know that."

I sat there a few minutes longer, itching to get back to the warmth of the Zooks' kitchen, just below us.

Then without warning, she jerked up. Stood right up and stared at something small and square in her hands. "*Himmel*, what's this?" she sputtered.

I hurried over to see what great treasure she'd just uncovered. "Looks like . . . is it a *picture*?" I asked, amazed.

"Well, goodness me, I don't rightly know." She rushed over to the lantern, and I followed.

There under the light, she held up a photograph of an

Amish man. It was old and tattered. Where it had come from, I had no idea, because Amish folk don't believe in such things as taking pictures of themselves. Especially the Old Order Amish, which Rachel's family certainly was.

"Who *is* this?" she whispered, eyes wide with wonder.

"Maybe your parents could tell you."

She turned to look at me, worry creasing her brow. "Now, don'tcha breathe a word of this to Dat or Mam, ya hear?"

I was startled. This was one of the few times she'd ever spoken so frankly to me.

"Okay," I replied. "We'll keep it secret."

She nodded, lowering the picture. "We hafta zip up our lips about this, honest we do. 'Cause I think I've stumbled onto someone. Someone who ain't too fondly remembered in these parts."

"Who?" I was dying to know.

"I think this here's Joseph Lapp . . . perty sure 'tis."

I inhaled sharply. "Our ancestor? The man who got himself shunned for marrying outside the Amish church?"

"It's beyond me why he thought he had to go off and marry his English sweetheart" was all she said. And I knew by the scowl on her face she meant business about not spilling the beans.

"Count on me to keep it quiet," I said. "Nobody'll hear it from *my* lips."

So it was settled. We had a secret between us. A big, juicy one.

"Why do you think your parents kept this photo all these years?"

Rachel shrugged her shoulders. "Dat probably knows nothing of it. Mam must've hid it, I'd guess." She shook her head, puzzled. "Looks to me like it's been passed down for generations. Really odd, though."

It *was* peculiar, to say the least. But even more intriguing was the inquisitive look on Rachel's face. Why her sudden interest in a shunned man, one who'd left the Amish church?

TWO

Esther Zook, Rachel's mother, was a devout and energetic woman who derived great satisfaction from the simple things: cooking, baking, caring for her children, and cleaning house.

Nearly every year, long as I could remember, she would throw a doughnut-making party, usually in mid-February. After all, it was the dullest, bleakest time of year, smack-dab in the dead of winter. Of course, Esther would never admit to calling it a party. Amish folk didn't engage in such "fancy" things. Still, it was a major event all the same.

Often on Valentine's Day—an icy Saturday morning *this* year—she liked to fill up her kitchen with close friends; her married sisters, too. Rachel and her younger sisters—Nancy, Ella Mae, and little Susie—were the ones most encouraged to join in the fun. And today was the annual doughnut-making day at the Zooks' old farmhouse, just across the meadow from my house.

This time of year, it was fairly easy to see the Zooks' place through the bare branches of the willow grove. The trees ran along the dividing line between our property and theirs. Only an occasional dried-up leaf clung to the wispy limbs.

I made my way down snow-packed SummerHill Lane, glad for fur-lined boots and gloves and my warm earmuffs. Pennsylvania winters weren't anything to scoff at. The sting in the wind was enough to turn my cheeks numb by the time I made the turn onto our neighbor's private lane.

Gray carriages galore were already parked in the side yard, their tops glistening with a hint of snow. The horses had been led to the barn for warmth and watering by Rachel's father, Abe, and her younger brother, Aaron.

"Come in, come in," my friend greeted me as the back door swung wide.

"Br-r, it's cold," I said, closing the door quickly and slapping my gloved hands together.

"Warm yourself by the stove," she offered.

"Thanks," I said, hurrying over to the large black wood stove, where Rachel's mother was keeping a watchful eye on the fryer.

"Glad you could come over and help." A dimple appeared in her cheek as she smiled.

"Nice to be here," I said, grinning back.

The kitchen smelled heavenly, of yeast and dough. My mouth watered with the aroma. "Mm-m, I can't wait for a bite," I told Rachel.

"Me neither." She took her mother's place at the stove, monitoring the oil in the fryer, making sure that it did not exceed the temperature needed to begin cooking the doughnuts.

Nancy, Rachel's thirteen-year-old sister, scurried

about taking my coat and hanging it on one of the wooden pegs in the outer utility room, just off the kitchen. "Now we hafta find you a spot to work," she said.

"Ready when you are," I said, tying on the long Amish apron handed to me by one of the women.

"There," Nancy said, stepping back to have a look at me. "Don't you look perty . . . and Amish."

I curtsied comically, and she laughed. Glancing around, I looked for Susie, the youngest Zook.

"If it's Susie ya want, she's kneading dough over there." Nancy motioned for me to follow her to the long wooden table.

Little Susie, now seven but still quite petite, was squeezing and punching at a big mound of dough. "Come and take a poke, Merry," she said, eyes sparkling.

I noticed her pretty blond hair, wound around her head in braids, and her long rose-colored dress and white smock-style apron. She was the cutest little Amish girl in all of Lancaster County!

I rolled up my sweater sleeves and folded Susie's piece of dough over and over. "How am I doing?"

She giggled sweetly. "Ya must've remembered from last year."

"Guess you're right," I said, looking up.

Across the enormous kitchen, Rachel was chattering in Pennsylvania Dutch. When she caught my eye, she waved at me, wiggling her fingers in midair.

"Have ya heard anything from Levi lately?" Susie asked.

I didn't respond immediately, thinking what I should say about her big brother's most recent letters. "He's been writing me every now and then. You have to remember, your brother keeps very busy with his classes this semester."

She nodded. "I miss him around here. Wish he'd come home for *gut*."

"I know you do."

"Maybe if ya say you'll marry him someday . . . maybe then he'll come back to SummerHill and stay put."

I had to chuckle. What she didn't know was that no amount of pleading could bring Levi Zook back to SummerHill. From me or anyone. He was right where he believed God wanted him to be—in Virginia, attending a Mennonite Bible college.

Besides, Levi and I had sort of come to an agreement about our friendship. That didn't mean he wasn't still "sweet" on me, as he would say, but we knew where we stood as far as romance.

The problem, of course, was my age. At almost fourteen and a half, I was in no way ready to be thinking of settling on a steady boyfriend. Especially one who was bound and determined to be either a Mennonite preacher or a missionary.

The reason being, I hadn't received a "call" to be a minister's wife. I was open to it, though. That is, if the Lord had something like that planned for my future. Still, I had all the time in the world—one of my mother's all-time favorite expressions when it came to boys and romance. But it didn't keep me from answering Levi's wonderful letters.

"When's my brother coming home for a visit next?" Susie asked.

"He hasn't said," I replied. "Honestly, I think you'll hear about that long before I do."

I sighed, thankful that Rachel was heading our way. Just in time to interrupt this awkward conversation.

She and her sisters and the other women began shaping the dough for frying. But nobody felt the need to stop talking. No, the chatter and the work seemed to flow effortlessly, as smooth and easy as the feel of the dough beneath my fingers.

In a matter of minutes, the deep-frying stage was complete. The youngest Zook girls were called on to create the creamy, rich frosting that would fill up the doughnut holes.

Susie and Ella Mae squealed with delight. They'd been given the honor of having the first taste test. I watched them smack their lips and lick their fingers.

"It's Merry's turn," Susie said. The adorable little girl stood in the middle of the kitchen, waiting for me to have a sample.

"Oh, it melts in your mouth," I said after my initial bite. And it did, literally. The deep-fried doughy treat and the gooey filling dissolved on my tongue.

Rachel came up behind me and whispered in my ear. "Still keeping our secret?"

"My lips are sealed," I replied.

"Gut, then. If ya keep that secret, then there's another one forthcoming."

I turned to face her. "About you-know-who?" I was referring to Joseph Lapp.

"No." She shook her head. "I'll tell ya later."

Her eyes shone, not so much with excitement as with a hint of apprehension. About what, I had no idea.

THREE

I was still wondering about Rachel's comment as I hurried home around noon, arms laden with a box of delicious homemade doughnuts. "You won't believe how truly amazing these are," I boasted to my mother.

"I'll be the judge of that," she said with a grin, opening the box lid.

I watched her munch on the first bite, her brown eyes popping. "What do you think?"

"Mm-m. Out of this world!"

"How'd we get them down here?" I teased, parroting one of the fun-loving phrases my father liked to say.

She went to rinse her sticky fingers at the sink while I placed the box of doughnuts on the kitchen counter. "Save some for Dad, okay?" I said.

"If we don't, we'll never hear the end of it," Mom said with a twinkle in her eyes. She reminded me that Dad had already been informed of today's Amish get-together. "He'll be thinking 'doughnut heaven' all day long, most likely."

"You're right," I said, pitying the poor emergency-room patients who might have to put up with his savory distraction.

Mom went to tend her African violets in the sunny corner of the kitchen. She pinched off an occasional leaf, commenting on the special plans I had for the afternoon and evening. "What time are your girlfriends coming for the Valentine's sleepover?" she asked.

"Around four. But don't worry, we won't need any food or entertainment."

"No supper?" She looked startled. "How can that possibly be?"

"Oh, we'll eat later on, for sure. It's just that Ashley and I have an agenda."

"I see," she said, without inquiring as to our plans.

Relieved, I picked up Lily White, my smallest cat, and carried her upstairs to my bedroom. As usual, Shadrach, Meshach, and Abednego followed on my heels.

"What have you been doing all morning, little boys?" I asked as the male cat trio made themselves at home on my bed.

Abednego had something to say. His eyes did the talking, and it seemed to me that he wasn't one bit pleased. Disgruntled was more like it.

"Okay, okay, I confess I enjoyed myself over at the Zooks' making doughnuts, but you know you're not supposed to be eating fattening, icky sweet things. S'not good for your health."

That didn't cut it. Shadrach got up and went over, plopping himself down next to Abednego. As if to say, *We're united on this sweets thing.*

"What can I say?" I shot back. "Cats as fat and sassy

as you have to cut back somewhere. Besides, Amish doughnut-making sessions are not meant for felines. Period."

Nobody was listening. Especially not Abednego, the fattest of the group.

Lily White, petite and demure, seemed to agree with me, however. But that was par for the course—she was always taking my side when it came to ganging up on the masculine animals in the Hanson household.

"Okay, if that's all there is to it, I've got work to do." I told them about the sleepover. "There'll be four young ladies here in this room tonight, so it will be a bit cramped with all of you hanging out. I want everyone on his best behavior. Hear?"

Abednego, the feistiest cat God ever made, closed his eyes slowly, deliberately. *We'll see about that*, I could almost hear him say.

"Better get a grip on your attitude," I shot back. To which he merely snoozed.

I set about cleaning my room, dusting and vacuuming. I wanted the floor especially spotless because we were going to roll out all of our sleeping bags. So we could be together. It was time for the women of SummerHill to unite.

The "English" ones, that is. I honestly couldn't see inviting the Zook girls over here. No chance they'd be allowed to come anyway. Abe Zook was a very strict father, following Amish church rules to a tee.

Ashley Horton, our pastor's daughter, and I had been planning this overnight event since right around New

Year's. Thank goodness Lissa Vyner and Chelsea Davis had agreed to come, too.

There was only one slight concern—Jonathan Klein—the reigning Alliteration Wizard. The boy I'd had a crush on forever and ever. Only thing, he'd decided now that it didn't really matter *who* he partnered with for his word games. Not anymore. So my idea to teach my girlfriends how to speak alliteration-eze wasn't something to worry about. It was a way to show him that our game didn't matter much to me, either. Besides, I wouldn't have to let Jon in on our secret plans. He'd find out soon enough. . . .

❧ ❧

Four o'clock, on the dot, the girls arrived.

"Listen to this," Chelsea said as we settled in to my bedroom. "Like lions, lizards lick their lips."

Ashley frowned. "Is that true? Do lizards have lips?"

All of us burst out laughing.

"That's not the point," I explained. "Chelsea just used mostly *l* words in her sentence. That's what alliteration-eze is all about."

Ashley nodded, her eyes wide with embarrassment. And I could see that getting through to her might be a chore.

"Does Jon Klein have any idea that we're meeting like this?" Lissa asked. She'd perched herself on my bed, cross-legged as usual.

"I sure hope not," I said. "But so what if he does?"

"Yeah, I'm with Mer," said Ashley. "What's it matter if he finds out?"

"He thinks he's so good at his little word game," Chelsea remarked. "Better than anyone around."

The girls looked at me. "Maybe Merry's the only marvelous mind," said Chelsea.

"Hey, you're getting the hang of it. Been practicing?" I asked.

She nodded. "My mother and I have been talking in alliterated sentences for fun around the house."

I was thrilled to hear it. Chelsea's mom was coming around, it seemed, and it was about time, too. She'd been through excruciating experiences, recently having been brainwashed by a bunch of weirdos—a cult group, to be exact. The nightmare had left her disoriented and shattered emotionally and spiritually.

"Good," I said. "Sounds like your mom's having fun again."

"Finally," Chelsea said.

We settled down to the task at hand. I gave out index cards and sharpened pencils to each girl. "Let's write ten words, either adjectives or nouns, using the first letter of your first name." I glanced at my watch.

"No time limit, please," Chelsea pleaded. "This isn't school."

Lissa nodded in agreement, her light blond hair brushing against her chin. "You've been doing this lots longer than any of us, Mer," she said softly. "We need time to catch up."

I figured they'd need plenty of practice. Guess this sort of thing came easy to some and hard for others.

Abednego and his brothers nosed their way either into

my lap or close by. Lily White snoozed high on my desk top.

Good, I thought. *They're on their best behavior.*

Watching the girls scribble down their word lists, I wondered if I was doing the right thing, letting them in on *my* thing with Jon. For the first time since Ashley and I had dreamed up this secret study session, I felt a twinge of regret. Was I really ready to kiss this game between Jon and me good-bye?

Chelsea's hand was in the air. "Oh . . . oh, teacher," she joked. "I'm ready."

I leaned back against the bed, pulling my knees up to my chin. "Read away."

She glanced around, almost sheepishly. "Here goes. 'Charming, cheery, chief, chicken, chime, chop, cheese, church, chum, chasten.' "

"It's genius," I said.

Ashley was nodding her head, eyes wide with near terror. "I can't do that . . . not so quickly."

"Okay, just keep working," I said, and we listened to Lissa's list next.

"Do I have to?" she asked, almost in a whisper.

I leaned forward. "Only if you want to."

She glanced around at our circle of four. "Okay, but nobody laugh, promise?"

We promised, and she read, " 'Light, long, laugh, limit, lash, Lord, lavender, loss, lanky, life.' "

Everyone clapped. "Truly terrific," I said.

She blushed purple. "Thank you."

Just then Lily White rolled off my desk, landing—*kerplop*—in Lissa's lap.

"Oh!" she shouted.

Quickly, amidst loud giggling, I ran to rescue my too-relaxed kitty. "Say sorry," I said in her ear.

Lissa grinned. "Don't worry, I'm fine."

"It's the cat Mer's worried about," Chelsea joked.

I placed Lily White on my bed. "That's not even close to being true," I reprimanded Chelsea. All three of the girls giggled gleefully.

Now . . . for the biggest challenge. Ashley Horton's word list. I was worried sick for her—about what she would or wouldn't come up with.

"Are you ready?" I asked her.

"I'll give it a shot." She touched her hair, laughing nervously. "Ashley starts with *a*, so I'll go with 'ashen, azure, alphabet, amazing, animal, accordion . . .' "

She stopped.

"Good start," I told her.

"That's all for now," she said, covering her index card with her hands.

I knew she was struggling. "Okay, the next thing we'll do is create sentences out of the words on your list."

"You've gotta be kidding," Ashley said.

Chelsea, on the other hand, went right to work. Lissa thought for a moment, then began to write.

"I'll help you," I said, sliding over next to Ashley.

"Thanks," she said, offering a smile. "You're a life-saver."

❧ ❧

In no time, Chelsea was dying to read her sentence aloud. And like it or not, she was inhibiting Lissa and

Ashley with her ability, but I couldn't stop her. Besides, it was fun to see someone blossoming under my tutelage.

"It sounds ridiculous, but here's what I have," she said. " 'A charming and cheery chief chopped a piece of cheese, chastened his chum the chicken, and headed for church when he heard the chimes.' "

Her sentence brought hooting and hollering. "She's better than Jon!" declared Ashley.

Chelsea beamed. "Thanks, but I still need practice."

"We *all* do," Lissa said, crumpling up her list.

"Time for tea," I said jokingly. It was time for a change of scenery, that was certain. Couldn't have my other students getting discouraged so soon.

I went to the door and opened it, calling down the steps. "Mom? Got any snacks?"

"Come on down, girls," she said. "There's plenty of whatever you like."

Thank goodness for food, I thought. And friends and family.

FOUR

The next day, Ashley, Chelsea, Lissa, and I sat together in Mr. Burg's Sunday school class. Chelsea and Lissa paid close attention. I was thrilled. Neither of them had grown up in church; both were new to the Gospel, Chelsea having declared herself an atheist years ago. Her heart had recently softened toward the Lord since the heartbreaking circumstances with her mother. Best as I could remember, she hadn't skipped a single Sunday morning service since her mother's return home.

After class, when Jon Klein came over to greet us, he pulled out all the stops. "Goodness, it's great to get God's gift going . . . and going."

"Sharing salvation's story?" I asked.

"Ah! Most moving, Merry, Mistress of Mirth," he said, flashing his big smile and brown eyes.

"*Must* you?" I said, teasing. Would he assign me a letter of the alphabet—*m* for instance?—in front of my girlfriends?

Mentally, I got ready for a montage of *m*'s while he showed off, alliterating left and right. But nothing was said about me joining in, and I realized we weren't even close to challenging him to an alliteration match as a group. He was way too good.

"Finally figured out fun stuff on my fantastic camera," Jon said, directing his comment to me at last.

"A fine thing for the faces of family and friends." I chuckled.

Ashley was watching me now. Had to be careful. I couldn't let on to her how important this alliteration thing was to me. She was just so . . . so *terrible* at it.

Anyway, Jon told us about the cool camera he'd received for Christmas, complete with telephoto lens—the works. Since my camera was very similar, I understood his enthusiasm.

"In fact," he said, "I'd like to focus on the four of you, maybe in the foyer later?"

"I don't mind," Chelsea spoke up. "Just do something creative."

"Yeah, like have us hug hymnals," I suggested.

His eyes lit up. "I have an idea. . . ." That faraway look seemed to take over.

"It's time for church to start," I said, cooling it with the alliteration. "I can't believe you brought your camera along."

He shrugged off my comment. "Let's meet in the coat room right after church," Jon said.

"It's a deal," Chelsea said, grinning.

Ashley and Lissa seemed hesitant.

"What's the matter?" I asked later. "It's just a couple of poses? So what?"

"We're hobnobbing with the enemy," Lissa said.

Chelsea was nodding her head. "Yeah, I thought we

were supposed to produce puns and provoke a parade of phrases, not *pose* for the pal."

"Great! You're getting good," I said, congratulating her and secretly wondering if she might not dethrone the Alliteration Wizard. Soon!

"So?" said Chelsea. "What about it?"

"Don't you see?" I told them. "By hanging around the Wizard, you'll pick up a lot. Just keep your ears open."

We walked down the aisle and sat in the pew right behind my parents. Mom and Dad turned around and greeted us politely. "You're welcome to have dinner with us," my mother told the girls.

They thanked her quietly for the invitation because the organ music was beginning to swell.

"We'll talk about it after church," I said, settling back into the comfortably cushioned pew. Mom was always interested in hostessing—*my* friends, *her* friends, and Dad's friends from the hospital. Leave it to my mother to assemble a group of people for the sole purpose of feeding them. She didn't live to eat—she lived to feed others!

I noticed how beautifully the church was decorated, with several bouquets of red and white roses. When I read the bulletin, I saw that three different families had donated flowers in memory of loved ones who'd passed on.

Briefly, I thought of Faithie, my own deceased twin, and wondered if she might've had the gift of alliterating had she lived past age seven.

I reached for the hymnal, eager to sing the songs with my friends—the old, inspired hymns of the church.

By the close of the service, I was curious about Jon

Klein's invitation for us to pose for pictures.

Why *had* he asked us?

❦ ❦

Ashley was all bubbly about the picture-posing session, and I assumed it was because she still had a crush on Jon. Not that I blamed her. Jonathan Klein was a cute guy. Though a teenager—our age—he seemed older, more studious, too.

Anyway, we met in the coat room. "Do you mind wearing coats?" he asked rather shyly. "We should go outdoors."

The boy was learning fast. Although it was high noon, the sun had been hiding behind clouds most of the morning, so Jon was wise. He'd probably been reading up on the best use of light. Which was, of course, just after sunrise or just before sunset. That's when the low sun casts a golden glow over everything—people, animals, and landscape.

We were all bundled up now, standing on the front steps. Ashley wore her new outfit, a red wool coat—very stylish—with a tam and gloves to match.

Lissa, on the other hand, wore a camel-colored hand-me-down coat I'd given her—clean and neat. Looking at her, I realized the full-length coat fit her far better than it had ever fit me.

Chelsea was wearing a big grin. "I didn't dress up much today," she said, eyeballing the rest of us. Hers was a cute down-filled ski jacket of blue and green.

"You're fine," I said, picking lint off my own teal blue dress-up coat. "Where do you want us, Jon?"

He had us line up on the church steps, single file. Like stairsteps. Lissa, being the shortest, stood on the bottom step. Next came Ashley, me, and on the very top step, Chelsea.

"Okay, let's have a serious pose," he said.

"Like we're proper, eighteenth-century ladies?" Chelsea asked, turning this way and that.

"Why not?" Jon replied. "Think *Little Women*."

Trying to be serious when you're told to be isn't the easiest thing in the world. So we attempted somber faces, but what followed were waves of hilarity. We sincerely tried to keep a straight face, just never quite succeeded.

Jon started snapping, whether we were ready or not. "Beautiful, ladies," he said, crouching down to get unique angles. His actions reminded me of the way I always liked to lean into my own picture-taking.

When Mr. and Mrs. Klein came out of the church, Jon's father expressed momentary astonishment, then motioned to his son.

"Uh . . . thanks, girls," Jon said, running to catch up with them.

"We're finished?" Ashley said. "Just like that?"

"And Jon didn't even alliterate once," Lissa moaned.

"That's okay," I whispered, "because we have lots of work to do before we'll ever get as good as he is at alliteration-eze."

"You're right," Ashley muttered.

I drew them into a huddle. "Who's coming to my house for dinner?"

Maybe the girls were afraid I'd make them recite alliterated phrases all afternoon. I don't know, but they all said they couldn't come.

"Thanks for a super sleepover, though," Ashley said.

I gasped. "Hey, you did it!"

"What?" she asked, wide-eyed.

"You used two *s*'s in a row. And without thinking." I gave her a big hug. So did Chelsea and Lissa.

"I guess all that brain strain is paying off," she said.

"Alliteration Wizard, move over!" Chelsea laughed.

We stacked up our hands, like we were making a promise or some sort of pact.

"Let's practice at school tomorrow," Lissa suggested.

"During lunch," said Ashley.

"Delectable decision," added Chelsea.

We waved and went our separate ways, scattering across the parking lot of the church. Mom was disappointed that my friends weren't joining us for another meal.

"Maybe I'll invite Rachel Zook over for dessert," I told her as we rode the short distance to SummerHill Lane.

"Oh, *would* you, Merry?" she pleaded. "It's been a long time since I've seen your Plain friend."

So it was settled. After dinner, I would go to the Zooks' and fetch our neighbor. Maybe Rachel and I would have time to talk privately. Then she could share her additional secret. The one she was so fired up about yesterday.

FIVE

By the time Mom's four-course dinner was served and eaten, it was beginning to snow again. Donning my warmest clothes, I headed out into the blustery air.

I plodded along the footpath that led from our back porch to the main road out front. Anticipation began to build in me, and I played guessing games with my imagination. What secret did Rachel have "forthcoming," as she'd said so evasively?

Pausing along the side of the road, where the ditch had filled up with snow, I tried to remember how the grassy slope looked in the summertime. "Warm days have flown," I said to the ground, lamenting the cold. My breath turned into instant ice crystals in the frosty Pennsylvania air.

Hurrying on, I breathed through my nose, wrapping the warm, woolen scarf around the lower portion of my face. I almost laughed out loud, suddenly realizing to what extent I was willing to go to satisfy my mother's need to be hospitable.

What if Rachel decided she didn't want to brave the elements and return with me for pie and ice cream?

Br-r. The thought of anything cold to eat made me shiver.

Surely she'd come, though. I was close to one-hundred-percent-amen sure she would. The off Sundays were a visiting day for the Amish. Today was one such day.

Unexpectedly, I spied Rachel's big brother Curly John up ahead. He was helping Sarah, his wife, out of their parked carriage. I had no idea how they'd arrived without me seeing them. They must've pulled into the Zooks' lane while I'd dawdled on the side of the road, daydreaming over summer, long gone.

I could scarcely believe my eyes. Sarah handed a long, blanketed bundle to Curly John. Realizing that this must be the former "baby Charity," the abandoned baby I'd found in our gazebo last July, I called to them. "Sarah! Curly John! Wait up." I scurried over the snowy lane to catch up.

They greeted me with warm "Hullos" and "Howdy-dos," then we hustled into the old farmhouse, where the Zook family was enjoying the afternoon in their toasty kitchen. Abe and Esther sipped hot coffee, while their children played games at the table and on the floor near the wood stove.

"*Wilkom*, Merry," Abe said, waving one of the children over to hang up my coat and scarf.

Almost instantly, the family gathered around the baby. They were drawn to her like bees to honey.

"How's our first grandbaby?" Esther cooed, taking Mary right out of Curly John's arms.

"She's really grown," I said, squeezing into the circle with Rachel on my right.

The children took turns kissing the little one's hand and touching her button nose ever so lightly. Even Aaron, the only boy there, stroked her rosy cheeks.

Sarah turned to me and smiled. "Our little Mary's such a blessing. We thank God every day that you found her and took such good care of her for us."

I hadn't seen Mary since I'd baby-sat for her at the end of last summer, before school started. "What is she now—nine months old?" I asked.

"Jah, you're right." Sarah helped her mother-in-law untangle the baby blankets, then asked, "Wanna hold her?"

Did I ever! I took one look into that adorable face and nearly cried as Esther placed her in my arms. "Oh, she's so beautiful," I whispered.

Mary tried to babble sweet baby words, probably some simple Dutch, raising her little hand up to my face to be kissed. The gesture took me back to that first night we'd spent together, this precious baby and me, when she'd curled her infant fist around my finger and squeezed with all her might.

Rachel's father was begging for equal time. "Come see your *Dawdy* Abe a bit," he said, slapping his knee.

I kissed her baby ear. Gently, I set Mary on her grandpa's lap, relinquishing her to his strong, loving arms.

Before I could blink an eye, someone had slipped a plate of warm apple pie and a hearty dip of ice cream into my empty hands. "Oh, uh . . . thanks, but—"

"Don'tcha want none?" Rachel asked, a quizzical look on her face.

"Well, I came to invite you for dessert at *my* house." We burst into laughter, standing near the rocking chair where Abe Zook played with his adopted granddaughter.

" 'Tis hard to fellowship with friends and not be feeding one's face, 'least not in an Amish household," Rachel said.

She was right about that.

"What'll I tell my mother?" I said. "You know how she loves to cook and entertain."

She nodded, eyes shining. "My mam and yours could do right fine together—opening up a restaurant somewheres," she admitted.

"That would never do."

"Why not?" she asked.

"Because *two* cooks in a kitchen are always one too many!"

We giggled about that, taking turns making over the baby. "Wouldn't Miss Spindler be surprised at how quick Mary's a-growing?" said Rachel.

"That's the truth," I said. "But you know how Old Hawk Eyes is . . . she probably saw Curly John's horse and buggy pull into your barnyard long before you ever did!"

"Probably so." Then Rachel's eyes softened, and she took my hand, leading me into the front room. "When you're done with your dessert, Merry, we hafta disappear for a bit, if ya know what I mean."

I must admit, I was thrilled. At long last, she was going to reveal her secret. Whatever it was.

"Wanna come to my house, then?" I whispered, glancing over my shoulder.

She nodded. "In a bit, we'll go."

My curiosity had been piqued. Still, it would take some doing to tear myself away from Rachel's darling niece—baby Mary.

To my surprise, Sarah Zook asked if I could help her out with Mary. "Occasionally, on Saturdays, just during quiltin' season mostly."

"I'd love to!" I said, putting on my coat and scarf.

"If you could come over to our place, that would help me an awful lot." She stepped into the utility room, where Rachel was struggling with her snow boots.

"My mother'll drive me, I'm pretty sure," I told her.

"Well, ask your momma, and just let Rachel know, jah?"

I said I would, yet wondered why she hadn't chosen someone Amish to baby-sit for her.

Rachel pulled on her boots with a grunt, then located her long gray woolen shawl on a crowded coat hook. "Ya noticed, didn'tcha, that my own sister-in-law didn't ask *me* to help with Mary," teased Rachel.

Sarah's cheeks blushed bright pink. "Oh, forgive me, Rachel. I would've asked, but—"

"I's just foolin' ya," Rachel replied. "How on earth can I hold a baby and do my best handstitchin', all at the same time?"

"Gut, then, you're not mad." Sarah offered a pleasant smile, then bid us "God be with ya's."

"Bye!" I called to her and now to Esther, who'd come to see us off.

Then before I could turn around, here came Nancy and Ella Mae, then little Susie, pushing her way against the storm door. "Where's Rachel goin'?" Susie hollered out.

"Oh, just over to Merry's for a bit," Rachel called back, a stream of her breath floating over our heads.

"She won't be gone long," I promised.

That is, if she spills the beans on her secret right off, I thought.

SIX

My mother was overjoyed to see Rachel. "Oh, here, let me take your wraps," she said, playing the ultimate hostess.

"*Denki*," Rachel said softly, removing her black outer bonnet and shawl. She glanced down at her feet nervously.

"Forget something?" I asked.

"Shoulda brought warm socks along," she whispered.

"Don't worry. I'll loan you a pair." And I proceeded to help her pull off her high snow boots.

Mom served up pumpkin pie a la mode, and Rachel and I ate it as if we'd never had any sweets at the Zooks'. After all, we were growing girls, and our eagerness pleased her mother to no end. Upstairs, we had my big bedroom all to ourselves. I'd straightened things up earlier from the sleepover last night. Even spent a few minutes smoothing out my comforter and reorganizing my CDs and knickknacks while Mom put finishing touches on our dinner.

"Ach, your cats have about taken over the place!"

Rachel remarked, looking around at the four of them as I closed the door.

I knew it was hard for her to accept mouse-catchers living the pampered life—inside the house. She'd always insisted that where they were *really* needed was outside, in a barn somewhere.

"I think you and my mother must have a conspiracy going about my pets," I told her, finding a pair of knee-length socks in my dresser drawer.

"Oh? What makes ya say such a thing?"

"Well, my mom put her foot down about taking in any more strays." I picked up Lily White and cradled her in my arms.

Rachel, watching me, smiled. "Maybe it's 'cause you treat 'um like they're babies."

I laughed. "Oh, but they *are* babies. Kitty-cat babies."

She shook her head, puzzled, then pulled out the chair beside my desk and sat down. "I hafta tell ya something, Merry, but ya must promise never to tell a soul."

I felt my forehead crease to a frown. "What do you mean?"

"Better sit down," she advised.

With Lily White in my arms and Abednego creeping closer, vying for his position as "Top Dog" kitty, I sat down on my bed and leaned against the bed pillows. "I'm listening."

"Gut, 'cause I need your help."

"*My* help?" Who was she kidding? Rachel Zook was one of the most resourceful teenagers around. Like most Amish girls, she could can peas and carrots to beat the band. She sowed the straightest rows of lettuce and tomatoes you ever did see and knew all about how to spring-clean a house up and down and inside out.

Not only that, she had a large hope chest just bursting with all sorts of essential linens and household items, ready to settle into keeping house and raising a family, which is what young Amish women did early on—when the right Amish fellow came along. Which was probably the case. She'd probably said "yes" to Matthew Yoder, her one and only beau. Probably wanted me to know before anyone else. . . .

Still, I dared not mention any of what I was thinking, only studied her solemn face and her folded hands as if she were about to pray.

"Well . . . do ya promise me, Merry Hanson?"

I took a deep breath before I answered. "I think you better say why you need my help. Then maybe I can make a promise."

Her eyes darted to the windows. SummerHill Lane could be easily seen from my bedroom, and right across from the road were acres and acres of field, now dormant.

I spoke up quickly. "I didn't mean to offend you, honest."

She looked my way again, making short little nods with her head. "Been ponderin' this for the longest time. I just hope ya won't think I've up and gone berserk."

Now I was really confused. "How could that be? You're smart as a whip, Rachel. Don't worry what I think, anyway. We're friends, right?"

"The best of friends," she said, looking truly inspired. She reached into her dress pocket and pulled out the old picture. The one of Joseph Lapp. I knew it was the same photo because the edges were yellowed and uneven.

Rachel stared at the picture in her hand. "I've been keeping a secret—a forbidden ambition—for ever so long, really. The People would be shocked and befuddled, especially my parents." She was almost whispering, and my heart went out to her, not knowing what she was thinking or feeling.

"Are you all right?" I asked.

"Don't rightly know" came the haunting reply. "I feel I may be ready to put some of my upbringing to the test."

I was worried. What could she be thinking?

"Oh, Merry . . . I wanna have *my* picture taken," she said suddenly, almost breathlessly. "It is the most vain, wicked thing I could possibly think of doin', yet I want it more than words can say."

"What about your Amish beliefs?" I asked.

"The People's opinions are not mine just yet. I must cast aside the Old Order rules for now," she said, explaining that she was now entering her *Rumschpringa*—the Amish term for the running-around years before baptism into the church and marriage.

During the mid to late teens, Amish young people are allowed to experiment with the outside world. Try on the various aspects of modern life and decide if Plain living is right for them or not. Most of them, in the end, choose to remain Amish and take the life oath at the time of their baptism.

"Are you completely sure about this? About having your picture taken?"

"Never more so," she replied. "Now . . . ya must be wonderin' how you could be helping me."

I'd already assumed she wanted me to be the one to take her photograph. And I was right.

"Dat and Mam are going out to Ohio to visit some relatives next weekend. I thought it might be a gut time."

I listened; didn't even nod my head to give consent.

"The moon'll be on the wane come Saturday night," she informed me. "We'll hide behind it, ya know."

I had to chuckle. She'd considered every possible angle.

"Then ya'll do it? Ya'll get out your camera and take my picture?"

"How can I?" I protested. "Knowing what your family believes . . . what your church teaches?"

"Making graven images?" she said. "Is that the problem?"

I moved my cats off my lap carefully and stood up. "Rachel, have you thought about the shame this could bring to your parents?"

"Ach, we've been through all this before," she answered. "A thousand times."

I realized she was talking about Levi now, her big brother. He'd gone off and embraced higher education, a no-no for Amish offspring. Of course, he'd nearly broken his father's heart by not joining the church at the appropriate age but leaving SummerHill and heading to Virginia—to a Mennonite college, of all things.

"Why put your parents through it?" I argued.

She looked at me, her eyes pleading. "You sound so Amish, Merry. You sure ya ain't?"

I laughed, which was probably a good thing. Our discussion was getting entirely too serious.

"Let's think about it. Don't rush into something you might regret later," I suggested.

She shook her head. "This could be my only chance, Merry. The only chance I'll ever have to see myself in a picture."

I leaned down and looked into the face of Joseph Lapp. "Guess my great-great-grandfather got something started, didn't he?"

She stood up, not looking out the window but at my wall gallery of framed photographs, some I'd taken of my twin sister long ago. "Please be thinkin' long and hard about this, Cousin Merry," she said.

I simply couldn't let her push me into this. And at the moment, I wasn't too receptive to being called her cousin, either. I had to admit, her obsession with vanity irked me.

"What about 'Children, obey your parents in the Lord'?" I said, picking up my Bible. "Does that count for anything?"

She whirled around. " 'Course it does! I've been following the *Ordnung* my whole life. Never once strayed from it, neither. But having my picture taken won't be disobedient to Dat and Mam . . . not really."

"Why not?" I asked, amazed at her logic.

"Because my *parents* never said not to."

"But the bishop and Preacher Yoder, what about them?" I had her. She couldn't shy away from the truth.

"Oh, Merry . . . please don't go makin' me feel worse than I already do."

"Okay, then. How about if I let you know what I decide in a couple of days?" I said at last.

"Gut," she replied, turning toward me. "We'll have my first and only picture taken in the barn."

"What?"

"You heard me," she said. "In the haymow."

Hadn't she listened to a word I'd said? I was truly flabbergasted, plain and simple.

SEVEN

Unfortunately, it wasn't as easy for me to stand my ground on Monday. Rachel showed up at the bus stop, first thing. She came running up the lane, waving at me like there was some emergency.

"Hullo, Merry," she said, out of breath.

"What're you doing here?" I glanced up the road for the bus.

"Didja think about it yet?" she asked, her cheeks red with the cold.

"Oh, that . . ."

"Jah, 'cause we need to start making plans."

"Well, I still don't think it's such a good idea."

"But you're my only chance, Merry," she said, eyes pleading, hands rubbing together.

"You could go into town and have your picture taken," I suggested. "That's easy enough."

"What . . . in one of them little booths with the black curtains?"

"Sure, why not?"

The bus was coming now. I could hear it rumbling before I actually saw it. I was positive she wouldn't want to be stared at by the public school crowd—I read it in the frenzied look on her face.

Darting her eyes back and forth between looking at me and surveying the crest of the hill, Rachel seemed nearly frantic. "Aw, Merry . . ."

"Better relax," I warned. "Go home, and we'll talk after school."

"I'll come right over then." She dashed off, her long skirt and apron flying under her woolen shawl.

"See you later!" I called to her, hoping I hadn't offended my friend.

"Jah, see ya," she replied.

❧ ❧

At lunch, Chelsea showed up with Lissa. I was already getting seated at a table with Ashley.

"Well, here we are together again," Chelsea said, salting her fries. "Has anyone seen the wizard today?"

"Not me," Ashley said.

"Not *I*," I echoed, correcting her English.

Ashley grimaced. "Where do you think he's hiding?"

I shrugged. "Jon never misses school—doesn't seem to catch colds much."

"True," Lissa said. "Wish I knew his health secret."

I laughed. "I think *I* know. He scares the germs away. As simple as that."

Ashley gasped. "You can't mean that, Mer. Jon's drop-dead gorgeous."

"Of course she didn't mean he was homely. Everybody knows Jon's cute," Lissa said. "*Very* cute."

"Ah, gotcha! Somebody's got a crush on the Wizard," I said. But my heart sank.

The four of us leaned on our elbows into the table, whispering comments about some of the other boys in our class. And that's the way we spent our time—eating and sharing girl talk.

When the first bell rang, Chelsea groaned. "Aw, we didn't practice our you-know-what."

"Oh well," said Ashley. "If Jon's out sick with the flu or whatever, he's lost a whole day of alliterating, too."

"What do you mean, *too*?" I reached for a napkin. "We haven't lost any time. Not really. Let's practice on other students—locker partners, teachers—you get the picture."

"Oh! Wait a minute," Chelsea blurted. "You just said something that reminded me where Jon might be."

I frowned, thinking back. "What did I say?"

"You said, 'Get the picture' . . . and I *do* know where the Alliteration Wizard is." She went on to explain that the basketball all-stars were having group shots made for the school yearbook. "Betcha Jon's taking pictures right now!"

"Let's check it out," I said. My girlfriends picked up their trays and followed me right up to the cafeteria window to deposit our empty trays and trash, then down the hall to the gymnasium. I felt like the Pied Piper of James Buchanan High.

"Sure enough," I said as we peered through the door to the gymnasium.

"There's our man," Ashley sighed, her hair falling down over her shoulder.

I didn't exactly know what to think of her comment, whether she meant it personally or what. But I realized anew that my commitment to teach these girls how to speak alliteration-eze was actually spilling over into my former romantic territory.

"Why are we spying?" I said at last, stepping back from the door.

"That's what I wanna know," Ashley spoke up. "We oughta be working on our secret language."

The final bell rang.

"Yee-ikes! We have three minutes to get to class!"

It must've looked mighty strange, all four girls scrambling off in opposite directions. But we did just that, and I didn't see Jon in any of the usual spots—not even at his locker—for the rest of the day.

❦ ❦

I did encounter Rachel Zook, however. She'd kept her promise and was waiting on my front porch, all bundled up in her Plain attire.

"Goodness, girl, what're you doing sitting out here in the cold?" I said, running up the steps.

"Waiting for my English cousin."

"C'mon." I grinned at her, and the two of us headed inside, arm in arm.

For once in a blue moon, Mom wasn't waiting with hot cocoa, freshly baked cookies, and a big smile as we entered the house. But my cat quartet was snug at home, and they came bounding down the main hall toward Rachel and me.

"Well, look at all of you," I said, bending down to pet each one.

Rachel put up with my fussing over the cats, though she seemed antsy to get on with what she wanted to discuss.

"Want something hot? A snack, maybe?" I asked.

"Hot chocolate's nice." She followed me down the hallway to the kitchen. There on the counter, I discovered a scribbled note.

Merry—

I mixed up some hot cocoa for you . . . there's a new batch of cookies in the pantry.

You mustn't worry when you read this. Daddy wasn't feeling too well this morning, so I'm heading to town to be with him.

Love you, honey,
Mom

I almost laughed—sarcastically, that is. "Don't worry, she says." How was *that* possible?

"What'sa matter?" Rachel asked.

Honestly, her words startled me. "Uh . . . I . . . my dad got sick, I guess," I told her.

"How sick?"

Suddenly, I was no longer interested in fixing a chocolate drink for either Rachel or myself. "Excuse me for a second," I said, heading to my father's study down the hall.

"I could come back another time," Rachel was calling to me from the kitchen.

"Just wait. I want to call the hospital." I hurried into

the study and picked up the phone.

Something's weird about this, I thought as I punched the numbers. When the hospital information person came on the line, I asked if Doctor Hanson had been admitted.

"Yes, he's in room 127. One moment, please." I thought she'd never connect me.

"Hello?" my mother answered, and I was truly relieved to hear her voice.

"Mom, what's going on?"

She sighed. "Oh, honey, it's been a frightening day, but Daddy's going to be all right."

"What do you mean? What happened?"

"I don't want you to worry about this, Merry," she said. "Your father's ulcer flared up again, but he's going to be fine."

"He *better* be," I mumbled, tears welling up. "Can I see him?"

"Not tonight, but soon. He's going to spend the night here . . . they'll be doing additional testing first thing in the morning." She sounded tired, and I knew I was pushing my luck to keep asking questions.

"Tell Daddy I love him," I said. "And you, too."

"I'll be home later, after supper sometime," she said. "There's plenty of food in the fridge. You won't starve."

"No problem, Mom, I'll warm up something. Count on me."

"Thanks, Merry. I'll see you soon."

I hung up. And oddly enough, I was actually aware of the steam whistling lightly in the radiator under the window next to me.

Pulling the curtain back, I looked out. The sky was

trying to show its icy blue face, but low clouds kept interfering, skimming across like white, wooly lambs chasing each other in the springtime.

"Oh, Lord Jesus, help my daddy," I whispered to the heavenlies. "Please . . ."

Quickly, I headed back to the kitchen and filled Rachel in, then set about making something to soothe us.

She played with the strings that hung down from her *kapp*, staring at the table. "Ya know, I think about things like this, Cousin Merry. That is, if something unexpected would happen to me, ya know."

"You're too young to worry like that! You're not going anywhere, Rachel Zook—I'm telling you right now."

She looked up at me, her voice shaky as she spoke. "I've actually worried what would happen if I died before—"

"Before what, Rachel? What on earth are you talking about?" I asked her sharply.

"There are certain things I wanna do. *Hafta* do. Not because I wish to hurt my parents or disobey the bishop. It goes clear deeper in me than any of that."

I suspected where she was going with this. "You're talking about the picture you want taken. Am I right?"

"Jah." She nodded her head again and again.

"Well, if it means that much to you."

She stood up suddenly. "Ya'll do it for me? Honest, ya will?"

I stirred her hot chocolate and placed it down on the

mat in front of her. "I'm your very own personal photographer."

I must've been out of my mind to agree to her wishes, but those no-nonsense blue eyes were far too serious to ignore. We were distant cousins, for Pete's sake!

EIGHT

My mother still hadn't returned home as I headed for bed. I'd finished all my homework, even chatted on the phone with Chelsea and Lissa for a while, practicing our word game a little—filling up the emptiness in the house.

I never mentioned a thing about Dad spending the night in the hospital. Just wasn't in the mood to talk to them about it, especially because I didn't really know what was wrong.

Welcoming the dark, I slipped into bed and pulled the sheets up around my head. Turning on my side, I held Lily White close. The freshly laundered smell of my pillow slip reminded me that most likely Mom was the one bearing the brunt of the day's trauma.

In many ways, she and I were alike. She took charge when there was a crisis, automatically it seemed. I was the same way. "Miss Fix-It," I'd called myself in the past. But I felt as if I might be mellowing a bit when it came to being such a rescuer.

Actually, in thinking about Rachel's request for a photograph, I should've refused. The "old" Merry might've. But I was feeling more adventuresome these days—since

Chelsea's mother had arrived home from the rehab center safe and sound—and, well, I felt it was time to change things about myself. Not that I'd be one-hundred-percent-amen successful.

Thankfully, it wasn't going to be a stormy night. It's hard to feel confident during a storm—makes you feel helpless, almost childlike. With my big brother, Skip, away at college and Mom becoming more involved with her antique collection, which involved some travel, I had to be at home alone at least occasionally.

So tonight I was thankful for a moon and a starlit sky. Feeling cozy under my comforter, I talked to God, expressing my concern for Dad. "Please let him know you're there with him, and bring my mother home safely. In Jesus' name, Amen."

I don't know why I didn't pray about Levi Zook, off training to be a minister, as I often did. Or ask the Lord to make it clear to me if and when I might receive a divine "call." The main thing on my mind tonight was the idea of being alone in this big, one-hundred-year-old house. Without Dad. And Mom somewhere between SummerHill and downtown Lancaster.

About the time my eyes were too heavy to keep them open, I heard the car pull into our driveway. Good. Mom was home. It was okay to give in to the sandman.

❧ ❧

The next morning at breakfast, Mom was full of talk. "It was like pulling teeth to convince your father to spend the night in the hospital."

"But the docs wanted to check him out, right?"

She nodded, looking perky for so early. "You know how he is."

I knew. In fact, I'd gotten some of my own stubborn streak from him. "Will he have to be more careful about what he eats again?" I asked, staring at the mountain of scrambled eggs and two pieces of toast on my plate.

"I wouldn't be surprised," she said, sitting down.

"Guess he'll have to start doing the cooking around here, then," I teased her.

"Meaning what?"

"Dad's just . . . uh . . . not as hung up on food, I guess." I almost added, *like you are.* But I was smart and kept my mouth shut.

"Well, along with adhering to a stricter diet, he's going to have to get out and exercise. I've been telling him for years, a brisk twenty-minute walk can make a big difference."

Mom oughta know. She was religious about her daily walks. Couldn't talk her out of walking even if a tornado was heading this direction, I didn't suppose.

❧ ❧

It turned out that Dad was given nearly a week off. But did he follow doctor's orders and rest? My father chose this period of time to get overly involved in my homework assignments. *All* of them. Meaning he stood over me as I worked. I should've been mighty glad about the academic hovering, I guess, but by Wednesday it was beginning to annoy me.

"Don't you have something else to do?" I teased, hoping he'd catch on. But he stayed right there in the kitchen, watching me work algebra problems, offering unsolicited assistance every few minutes.

"Dad, I'm fine. I *know* how to do this."

He blinked and frowned. Before I could stop him, he stood up and left the room.

"This is truly horrible," I muttered, getting up to go to find him.

He was in the living room, reclining on the sofa, eyes half-mast. I sat down across from him, wondering what to say, wishing I could unravel the last few minutes.

"I'm sorry," I whispered.

He looked up at me and smiled. "Don't worry, sweets. I'm just an old man twiddling his thumbs, anxious to get back to work."

"Better take care of yourself, though, don't you think?"

He nodded. "Can't do much else around here."

"Yeah, well, we wanna keep you kicking for a bunch more years."

He chuckled. "Don't you worry about that. The Lord's got plenty of work for me to do before they put me out to pasture."

"Oh, Daddy, don't talk that way. You're not a cow, and you're not old."

"Fifty years . . ."

I could tell he was struggling with his latest birthday. A milestone event. Couldn't even begin to imagine having that many candles on my cake. Still, I needed to cheer him up.

"Think about this," I said, pulling something out of

the air. "What would it be like never having had your picture taken?"

"My whole life?" he said. "Well . . . sounds to me like you've been talking to some Amishman. Now, am I right?"

I couldn't blow Rachel's secret. Best be careful what I said from here on out. "Is it a sin for them to pose for a camera?"

"All depends how you look at it." He laughed at his pun, then went on to explain the reason for their interpretation of the biblical commandment. "Many Plain folk believe that it is sinning against God to have pictures made of themselves. It's included in their view of 'the graven image.' "

"But is it *really* a sin? Or just thought to be?"

He shook his head. "In my way of thinking, the only way it's a sin would be to worship the photograph—let the picture come between the person and God."

"Makes sense."

"So . . . whose picture are you thinking about taking?" he asked, grinning.

I couldn't believe it. He knew me too well.

"Guess that's all I better say for now." I got up and stood beside the chair. "Need anything before I get back to my math problems?"

He waved me on, smiling as if he'd seen through something top secret. Which, of course, he had.

Rachel would clobber me good if she knew!

NINE

By the time Friday evening rolled around, I was actually looking forward to sneaking off to Zooks' hayloft with Rachel. I needed a break from my dad, and he from me.

I'd never participated in a picture-taking session like this before, and I wondered how things would play out. Originally, Rachel had said she wanted only one picture of herself, but when I explained that most photographers take ten to fifteen poses in order to get one *good* shot, she quickly agreed.

Silly girl! I was turning her into a debutante.

The moon was only half full as we approached the barn door. A few stars shone through stark tree branches to the east. If I hadn't known better, I might've thought the night was just a bit spooky, but Rachel wouldn't be thinking such a thing. She urged me on, lantern in hand, eyes wide with anticipation.

"This is your big night." I made small talk, conscious of the shoulder strap on my camera case as we hurried up the ramp of the two-story barn.

The wide wooden door creaked open as we pulled on it, then, silently, we stepped into the sweetest-smelling place in all the world. The haymow.

"I'm glad you picked this setting," I told her.

"Oh? Why's that?" she asked.

"It's beautiful, that's why." I looked at her all dressed up in her Sunday-best Amish dress and shawl, her winter bonnet nestled over the top of her devotional kapp. "And tonight, you look pretty as a picture."

A flicker of a smile crossed her face, then she looked more serious again. "I wanna let my hair down in one of the pictures," she announced.

"You what?"

"It's all right. Nobody'll ever know."

I shook my head. "People will know. *I'll* know . . . and so will the person who develops this roll of film." I studied her, my eyes beginning to squint. "Are you absolutely sure about this, Rachel?"

She didn't answer, just went over and stood next to a bale of hay, leaning on it. "Here's a gut place for the first one," she said, a hint of stubbornness in her voice.

"Sit down right there, why don't you." I pulled my camera out of its case. "And smile, okay?"

She posed and smiled, all right. I, on the other hand, felt a bit sad as I clicked away. Not because she was doing anything truly horrible, as far as I could tell. No, I was down in the dumps because she seemed to be changing—my long-time friend was definitely different the past few days. She was changing into a young woman with thoughts and ideas; plans that nobody in her entire household would ever agree with. Maybe not even Levi, her so-called wayward brother.

After many shots and numerous poses, I watched, stunned, as she removed her outer head covering and then the white veiling beneath. She didn't ask me to hold the sacred symbol, and for that, I was grateful. Rather, she placed it inside her dress pocket, then quickly took the bobby pins out of her bun.

Like a waterfall, the light brown hair cascaded over her shoulders, past her waist. She stood there smiling as though she'd already accomplished something mighty important. "There, now," she said. "I'm ready for the last picture."

"I hope we're doing the right thing," I muttered.

"Don't be questioning this, Merry." The way she said it, so sharply, sounded as if she were reprimanding me.

But I aimed and focused, recalling the days when I was fascinated with taking "before and after" pictures of people and things. Hoping this new look of Rachel's wasn't an indication of things to come, I finished up the final shot.

"Done," I said, packing up my camera equipment.

"Denki." She wound up her hair and put the veiling back on her head. "It's getting cold."

"It's *been* cold," I replied, wondering what delicious thoughts and ambitions had kept her warm during the entire picture-taking session.

"Now what?" she asked.

I looked at her, trying to see the real Rachel, my dear Amish friend. "What do you mean?"

"Wanna come to the house?" she asked.

We made our way over the particles of hay that dusted the wooden floor. I helped her close the barn door before answering. "What'll I do with my camera?" I reminded her.

"Jah, that's a problem."

"So I guess we oughta say good-night," I suggested, feeling a bit reticent with her now. As though I didn't know what to say next.

"Supposin' you're right."

It was an awkward moment, and even more so because I spied little Susie leaning out the back door. "Looks like somebody's missing you."

"I best go in." She reached for my hand and squeezed it. "I'll never forget this, Merry." And she was gone, running across the yard to the house.

I stood there watching from the moonlit shadows, listening as the two of them chattered away in their Amish tongue—Pennsylvania Dutch.

Soon, though, the storm door slammed shut and the animated talk faded. I was glad for the flashlight in my pocket. Amish barnyards were such dark places at night. Except for the pale light of the February half moon.

My parents would be waiting. I'd told them I was going to visit Rachel. Dad, bless his heart, had had the most comical look on his face. Of course, Mom had no way of knowing what the cheesy grin was all about. But I suspected he'd shared the vague secret with her while I was gone.

Hurrying up the drive toward SummerHill Lane, I glanced back at the barn, now dark. We'd hid behind the moon, all right, just as Rachel had said. And no one—no one in her Amish community, at least—was ever to be the wiser.

I expected a prick at my own conscience but felt no guilt. Dad was right, I supposed. Wasn't a sin at all to have your picture made.

 TEN 

The next day was Saturday, and I'd agreed to babysit for Mary while Sarah Zook hosted a work frolic—a quilting bee—in her home.

I arrived early, before the many horses and carriages I knew would be making their way to the Amish farmhouse. Sarah seemed delighted to have me come so soon and opened the door with a warm greeting and a bright smile. "Ach, Merry, gut to see ya," she said. "Come in and get yourself warmed up."

I followed her inside to the front room, which was sparsely furnished: two matching hickory rockers similar to the ones in the Zooks' farmhouse, brightly colored handmade rag rugs and throw rugs adorned the floor, and a tall, pine corner cupboard, displaying Sarah's wedding china set—typical for Old Order Amish homes.

But the thing that captured my attention was the large quilting frame set up in the middle of the front room.

Sarah must've noticed me eyeing the frame and the chairs set up around it. "We'll be making a quilt for Rachel today," she explained.

"Really? For Rachel?" I wondered if the womenfolk

who were coming to piece the quilt together might suspect that Matthew Yoder was courting my friend.

I thought back to last night and the many pictures I'd taken of Rachel. I hoped I hadn't thrown things off kilter by agreeing to photograph her, because this quilting bee seemed ripe with purpose. Was the soon-to-be-made quilt designated for Rachel's hope chest? Was this church district holding its collective breath for another wedding come next fall . . . or the next?

Thankful that Rachel was still young, but not too young to consider being courted, I wondered if she was feeling pressured. Was this the reason she wanted to "sow wild oats"?

Sounds in the kitchen—baby babblings—brought me back to my responsibilities at hand. "Mary must need some company," I said, anxious to see the little dumpling.

Quickly, Sarah led the way, calling to her baby daughter as we hurried to her. "Ya know it's your English friend, now, don'tcha? Do ya know your favorite sitter is here?" She leaned over and lifted Mary up, then handed her to me.

"Well, hello again, sweetie," I cooed into her big blue eyes. What fun I was going to have!

Almost on cue, she nestled her head against my shoulder. "Ah, she's a bit droopy," Sarah said, offering a blanket and a bottle. "Thank goodness, she ain't cranky. It's 'bout time for her mornin' nap, but ya just never know. Mary doesn't like to nap all that much anymore. Likes to be up and about, watchin' what everybody's doin'. 'Specially at a quilting."

I kissed the soft cheek. "We'll just rock a little, then.

How's that?" I suggested to my precious bundle, heading for the rocker in the corner of the kitchen.

"Ya'll see what I mean," Sarah said, grinning. "She's a live wire, that one."

I hugged Mary, wondering what I was in for today. She didn't seem restless just now, but I smiled to myself, thinking that maybe, just maybe, this baby felt comfortable with me, the girl who'd first found her.

Choosing to believe that, I sat down to rock the doll baby in my arms. A beautiful, live baby doll, dressed in light blue homespun linen.

❧ ❧

One by one, and sometimes in groups of twos and threes, the quilters began to arrive. Rachel Zook and her two grandmothers came in together.

When she spied me, she hurried over. "Whatever ya do, don'tcha leave till we have a chance to talk." Her eyes looked hollow, almost as if she hadn't slept much.

"You okay?" I asked.

"Jah, fine . . . fine. But it'll hafta wait" was all she said.

Now I was really curious. Was she having second thoughts about last night? About destroying the film maybe?

She scurried back to greet the women as they came into the kitchen. Most of them stood near the fire, warming their hands.

I watched Rachel, wondering why she hadn't even glanced at her little niece, now almost asleep in my arms. What could be so important for her to ignore baby Mary?

Snatches of gossip, this and that, filled the room. One group of women was discussing the weather in Dutch. I was pretty sure I was right because I recognized the word *Winderwedder*, meaning winter weather.

Closer to me, Dutch was mixed freely with English. An elderly woman was estimating the gallons of apple butter left over from one of the last work frolics. At least, I *assumed* that's what she was saying.

Without being noticed, I got up and put Mary in her playpen to nap, covering her with one of several beautifully hand-stitched baby quilts. Standing there, looking down at her pretty hair, I wondered how on earth she could sleep through the din of kitchen chatter.

But she did—twenty-five minutes longer than Sarah said she would. By the time Mary was awake again and ready to play with wooden blocks, I had gotten quite an earful of Amish hearsay.

So-and-so's cousin was found to have a portable radio in his courting buggy, and what was the preacher gonna do about it?

And would Naomi's Jake ever get himself baptized and join the church? Foolish boy. . . .

I had to be careful not to chuckle. The air was thick with conversation, and soon I had the notion that the faster these women talked, the faster their stitching needles worked the fabric.

Mary was drooling and giggling now as she knocked down the tower of blocks I'd made. I reached over and tickled her under the arm. She burst out with more cute cackles.

"I think you need a constant playmate," I said to her, rebuilding the blocks.

Unexpectedly, there was a break for the ladies, and everyone got up and had a snack of hot black coffee and sticky buns.

Rachel came over and sat down on the floor next to me, watching the block-building process only briefly before she spoke. "I've been thinking," she said softly.

"That'll get you in trouble," I snickered.

She placed her hand on my arm. "No, listen . . . I ain't jokin'."

I turned to her. "What is it?"

"Last night . . . remember?"

I nodded, glancing at the women milling about the kitchen. "Aren't you afraid you'll be overheard?"

"Nobody's payin' attention just now," she replied. She steadied one of the baby's blocks, pausing, then continued. "I wanna take things a step further."

I knew better than to respond, so I kept quiet, listening.

"Don't say no just yet, Merry. I wanna come to your house later and talk about attendin' school with ya."

"What?" I whirled around, knocking the blocks down accidentally. "Are you crazy?"

"*Monday*, that's when I wanna go to high school." Her voice was sure, but her face was gaunt. My friend had lost sleep over this latest wild idea of hers.

"This Monday? Two days from now?" I squeaked out.

"Jah."

Before I could say more, she got up. Went to pour some hot cocoa for herself.

"Yee-ikes. I think your aunt Rachel's gone ferhoodled," I whispered to tiny Mary.

And there we sat—the baby and I—mouths gaping, block tower scattered.

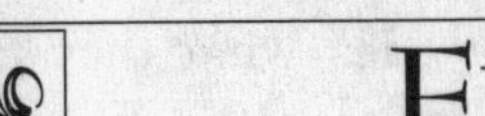

ELEVEN

After the quilting, Rachel and I continued our conversation at my house. "There's no way, Rachel. You can't do such a thing!" I insisted.

"Don't say I can't," she retorted. Her eyes were a hot blue flame, her neck growing redder with each second. "What'd be so wrong with me comin' with ya to your school? I'll be your visiting cousin, just for one day."

I couldn't believe what she was asking, what she was putting me through. Shaking my head, I sat on the floor, leaning against my bed.

Rachel, on the other hand, was making a beeline for my walk-in closet. "Could I borrow something to wear?" She didn't wait for my answer, just started taking things out of the closet and holding them up for me to see.

I groaned. "Oh, now I *know* you've flipped out!"

"Jah, flipped," she muttered, turning to look at herself in my dresser mirror. "Do ya have any idea how long I've been waiting to do this? A very long time, Merry."

I watched as she rummaged through more of my winter clothes. "What's this world coming to? My very own Amish girlfriend's losing touch with reality."

She agreed with me, smiling. "You can say that again. I'm a-tryin' on the English life, starting with *your* designer jeans."

"But, Rachel, do you have any idea what they feel like? They're tight, they're confining—not like the comfortable flowing skirts you're used to. And—"

"Still, I hafta know," she interrupted.

My hands flew up in surrender. "Okay, okay, try on anything you like." I hoped by my giving in, she'd give up.

The most astonishing smile swept over her face, and for the first time in a while, she looked well rested and serene.

"You mean it, Merry? You'll let me?" she asked.

"I said you could try on some clothes. That doesn't mean I'll pass you off as my 'English' cousin come Monday."

She shrugged her shoulders, as if to say *we'll see about that*.

❧ ❧

One thing led to another, and next thing Rachel was putting on some light pink lipstick, then mascara, fumbling with my eyelash curler in her hand.

"No . . . no, let me show you." I took the cosmetic bag from her. "Watch me."

Her curiosity couldn't be quelled, it seemed. And we spent nearly two hours making her over. Everything from curling the uneven ends of her long, long hair to brushing it straight back, attempting to hide the middle part.

Meanwhile, she did her best to persuade me. "Please,

Merry, won'tcha at least *think* about takin' me to your school?" She seemed eager to ride the school bus, for some odd reason. "I hafta see for myself what I've been missin'."

I sighed. "Oh, Rachel, what'll I do with you?"

She grinned. "You're gonna do it, that's what. Just this once, honest. Then I'll hush up about it."

I stared at her. She actually looked like any other teenager around Lancaster County with her makeup and long hair tastefully done. Well . . . close.

"I've turned you into a modern girl. A fancy one," I told her as she gazed into the mirror, turning the hand mirror at just the right angle to see the back of her hair.

"Jah."

"So what do you think?" I asked. "Like the new you?"

She went to sit on the bed, twiddling her thumbs in her lap. "I think I do." She was beaming. "Jah, I do."

I crossed the room to my closet and closed the door. "That's what I was afraid of."

"There's only one thing," she said. "I wanna wear my veiling over my new hairdo. Like a Mennonite."

"Okay with me."

"Gut, then," she said, grinning. "I'll go Plain, just not Amish."

"Better tone down the eye makeup and lipstick."

She groaned. "Must I?"

"Do you want to go to school with me or not?"

I had her over a barrel. She had no choice.

❧ ❧

I couldn't tell a soul—not even the tiniest part of my

plan with Rachel. She'd sworn me to secrecy, not that an Amish girl would know how to do such a thing as swear, but I'd promised, at least. And that was saying a lot about the whole situation. Because I knew without question this was most likely going to snowball. Might lead Rachel down a completely different life path—a too-modern one. But she was a mighty stubborn girl, determined to have herself a taste of English life, come what may.

TWELVE

My dad stayed home from church on Sunday. He wasn't feeling sick, he said, just not quite up to par. Because of that, I insisted on staying home, too. And then, because Mom was worried about Dad, she stayed home to oversee both of us.

I went around the house, upstairs and down, taking pictures of my parents. One of my mother cooking dinner, wearing her lacy apron. Another of her pouring milk into the cats' community bowl.

While Dad read his Bible silently, I took a shot of him from close up. He blinked his eyes and shook his head. "Can't you give a person fair warning?" he grumbled good-naturedly.

I laughed. "That would spoil everything, now, wouldn't it?"

He pretended to be blind for a second.

"Okay, I'm giving you advance notice this time. Don't move, just freeze," I said.

He cooperated, but it seemed that he was holding his breath, not blinking an eyelash.

I sat on the floor, angling the lens to get just his upper

torso. "There," I said when I'd finished, "that'll be an interesting perspective."

He glanced down at me. "Not half so interesting as your photo shoot with Rachel, eh?"

"Dad, what are you talking about?"

Returning to his Bible, he smirked. "You heard me."

"Oh, you don't know . . ."

He peered over his reading glasses. "Better not lead your girlfriend astray."

"How could that be?" I wailed. But I was disgusted with myself. Wished I hadn't given in to Rachel's request. And I wished something else, too: that my father didn't have eyes in back of his head!

"Let's have a devotional time," he said, calling Mom into the living room. "We'll have house church today—like the Amish do," he teased, sending a wink my way.

We took turns reading the Scripture references out loud—first Mom, then me, and last, Dad. I listened as my father read the devotional story, but the lesson didn't pertain to my dilemma with my friend. Rachel Zook was on my mind in a very heavy way.

While my mother prayed aloud, I did so silently. *Dear Lord, what should I do about Rachel?*

It didn't take long for the answer to arrive. Although I wasn't so sure it was a divine one. Rachel herself showed up after dinner. Came right into the driveway and parked her parents' horse and carriage.

"Wanna go for a ride?" she asked just as I answered the front door. "It's a right perty day for it."

I knew something was up because I noticed a twinkle

in her eyes. She was anxious to twist my arm some more about going to school.

"Come in," I said. "The kitchen's not quite cleaned up."

"I don't mind waitin'," she said, tiptoing into the living room.

Big mistake!

Dad was sitting in his favorite chair, reading. Actually, he was closer to snoozing than anything. But he opened his eyes wide when he saw Rachel coming, and I hoped he wouldn't question her.

"Well, hello there, Rachel," I heard him say as I hurried off to the kitchen. The sooner I finished up the kitchen, the quicker I'd have her out of there!

Things took a strange turn, though. Just as I was wiping off the counter tops, Jon Klein called. "I wanted to see if you were sick or something," he said, emphasizing the *s*'s.

"I'm not, but my dad's feeling a little out of it," I said.

"So . . . your SummerHill sisters started getting sassy. Silly too."

"Who're you talking about?"

"The tongue-twisting trio," he replied.

"Oh, Chelsea and company?" I should've known.

"None other."

I was curious to know what they'd said. "What did I miss?"

"Missed much, Mistress Merry." He was laughing. "They want a match. A meeting of the minds."

"When?"

"In a week."

"Says who?"

"Chelsea Davis got it started," he said. "She's getting good, Mer. You're a terrific teacher."

"Whatever." I was disgusted. My friends had jumped the gun. Hadn't waited for me to give the signal. They weren't even close to ready for a face-off with the Wizard.

"Hey, you sound upset. Everything okay?" His voice was sweet and mellow. Any other time—for instance, the months *before* I'd ruined things and divulged the alliteration game to my girlfriends—I might've delighted in his complimentary approach.

But now? My ability to pass on alliteration-eze was at stake.

"Fine, fabulous, fantastic," I replied.

"Yes!"

"Don't get worked up about it," I told him. "I'm not playing your game today. I'm too busy."

"Is this a bad time?"

"I'll talk to you at school tomorrow," I said.

And that was the end of it. We said good-bye and hung up. I marched into the living room.

"Well, it's good to see you're through with kitchen duty," Dad said, closing his book.

I eyed the two of them suspiciously. "Are you ready, Rachel?"

"Jah. Are you?"

"Sure am." I hurried to the hall closet to get my jacket, wondering what Dad had weaseled out of Rachel. "Let's go," I said, opening the front door.

"Your pop's awful funny," she said as we headed for the gray carriage.

"He *can* be," I said, getting in and sitting to her left.

She situated the woolen lap blanket over the two of us, then picked up the reins. "Why'dja tell him about taking my picture?"

I spun around, staring at her. "What?"

She didn't repeat herself.

"I didn't tell him, Rachel. I *didn't*!"

"Then how'd he know?"

I sighed. It was going to be a very long ride.

THIRTEEN

All the talk in the world wasn't going to convince Rachel to stay home on Monday morning.

Bright and early, she showed up at my house. "Plenty of time to change into modern clothes," she said when we were alone in my room.

"Do you honestly have to do this?" I whined.

She shook her head. "Can't talk me out of it."

Since I knew I couldn't, I started filling her in on life at public school—the teachers, the students, even the lockers.

"Lockers?" she gasped. "They have freezer lockers in a school? Whatever for?"

I couldn't help but laugh at her naiveté. "School lockers aren't for storing a side of beef or frozen vegetables, silly girl. They're for books and notebooks . . . and hanging up jackets and other things," I explained.

Eyes wide, she said, "Oh, I see."

Of course, she didn't comprehend; she couldn't possibly understand till she laid eyes on the whole setup.

I tried to prepare her for the crammed hallways, kids rushing to and fro, talking and calling to each other. "It's nothing like an Amish one-room schoolhouse," I said, brushing my hair. "There are just so many kids."

"What about higher learning?" she asked, pulling on a pair of my best jeans. *Designer jeans.*

"What?"

"Ya know, education past eighth-grade level. What about that?" she inquired.

"There's nothing magical about going past the eighth grade. If you're gonna be a good Amish girl, you can't be thinking about such things."

"Ya, I know. Still, it's awful tempting." Now she was standing beside me in the mirror.

"Don't tell me," I said. "You want me to do your hair like before."

"Would ya, Merry? Please?"

If I wanted her to be halfway accepted by "English" teenagers, I'd have to do something with her long locks. Short of cutting her hair, I knew there had to be a more becoming style, at least for a day at James Buchanan High.

"What about a French braid?" I suggested.

She grinned, showing her gums. "Whatever that is, I don't rightly know, but it sounds mighty nice. Foreign too."

I chuckled. "It's mostly American, I guess you could say. Don't worry, nobody's gonna mistake you for a French girl."

"*Puh!*" she said, and we had a good laugh.

Thankfully, she'd already eaten breakfast at home, so we were able to bypass the kitchen on our way out the front door.

Mom was busy in her sewing room, so I put a finger to my lips, signaling Rachel to be discreet. I'd told her to meet me at the bus stop. While I went to say good-bye to my mom, Rachel crept down the hall to the entry and outside.

"What's Rachel want so early?" Mom asked as I tried to wave to her and leave.

"What?" I said.

Mom looked up, needle poised in midair. "You heard me. What's Rachel doing over here?"

I couldn't tell her the ridiculous plan. She'd put her foot down; I knew she would. As I contemplated the situation, I realized that I was actually looking forward to taking Rachel to school with me, showing her around, introducing her to "what she'd missed."

But I had to get past my mother first, who'd obviously smelled a rat, and that wasn't just a joke. She was on to something.

Standing up, she came to the doorjamb and leaned out into the hall. "Where is she?"

"Rachel left already." It was true.

"Oh, so that's the end of it."

"The end of what?" I said, wishing I hadn't taken a bite of her bait.

She frowned, looking at me with inquisitive eyes. "From what your father says, Rachel Zook is walking a tightrope between Amish and English. He—uh, *we* don't think you should be the one to assist her in this spiritual journey."

"I'm not trying to influence her in any bad way."

Mom put her hands on both my shoulders. "Oh, honey, I don't mean to accuse you. Please don't misunderstand. We want you to continue being a good friend to her."

"But the best of friends put up with weird things sometimes," I said, hoping Mom wouldn't read anything into my comment.

"You're right about that. And I know you'll do the right thing by Rachel Zook."

My heart was beating ninety miles an hour. I knew if I didn't leave soon, I might start blurting out some of the top-secret plans Rachel and I had together in order to defend myself.

Fortunately, I heard the familiar grinding and groaning of the school bus. Rachel would be freaking out about now, wondering why I wasn't coming.

"There's the bus, Mom. Gotta run."

"Have a good day," she called after me.

"Thanks, I will."

Hopefully, it *would* be a good day.

❧ ❧

First off, Chelsea wanted Rachel and me to sit with her on the bus. This came as no surprise. I always sat with Chelsea. Besides that, she probably remembered Rachel from a brief visit last fall, when the Zooks had given her one of their puppy litter—a golden-haired cocker spaniel.

I was curious if Chelsea would recognize my "cousin" today, all done up in fancy clothes.

"This is Rachel, my neighbor," I said.

Chelsea did a double take. She studied her, then glanced at me. "You're Rachel Zook?" she whispered.

"Jah," said my Amish friend.

"Say 'yes' instead," I advised her. "And please remember to say it all day."

Chelsea was beginning to frown, leaning forward in her seat to survey the situation. "You're not saying—"

"Yep," I interrupted. "And it'd be best if you just play along. Know what I mean?"

"Hey," she laughed. "You're the boss!"

Relieved that she had agreed to cooperate and keep things under wraps, I talked softly to Rachel, hoping I'd covered everything necessary. "The main thing is not to worry about taking tests or doing homework assignments. Teachers won't expect you to participate. You're an observer, just visiting. Don't forget, okay?"

"Jah . . . I mean, yes."

She was catching on fast.

❧ ❧

The biggest hurdle was to get past Miss Fritz, our gregarious school counselor. She was known to roam the halls, greeting students by their first names, always eager to visit with new kids and their parents. Miss Fritz especially liked to meet visitors to the school. Actually, you were required to check in with her about any student who was *not* enrolled at James Buchanan High. A standing rule.

The second snag in getting Rachel through the halls and safely into my homeroom would be Jon Klein and his usual pre-class routine.

With Miss Fritz and the Alliteration Wizard on my mind, I guided Rachel through the labyrinth of hundreds of students, pointing her in the direction of the counselor's office. "Don't ask questions, just follow me," I instructed. "I'll do all the talking."

Rachel seemed content with taking it all in. She

scanned the rows of lockers, the banners on the wall, the water fountain, everything. There was a big smile on her face as we made the turn into the school office.

Miss Fritz was standing at her post near the attendance office, monitoring students with absentee slips and early dismissal permission slips. She was beaming as we came in.

"Good morning, girls," she said, glancing at Rachel, then back at me.

"Miss Fritz, I'd like you to meet my cousin Rachel. She's visiting school for the day," I said.

"Welcome to James Buchanan High School." Miss Fritz extended her hand. "Nice to have you, Rachel."

My heart pumped extra hard as they shook hands.

"How long will you be staying in Lancaster?" asked the counselor.

Rachel looked at me, obviously unsure of herself.

"Oh, she's from right here . . . out in the country, really."

"Whereabouts?" came the question I'd dreaded.

"SummerHill," I spoke up on Rachel's behalf.

I was one-hundred-percent-amen sure what the next question would be. *Well, then, Rachel, why aren't you in school?* she might ask.

Waiting for the inevitable, I realized I was holding my breath. *Relax*, I told myself.

The worst thing that could happen was for Rachel to be asked to leave, to go home. *Where she oughta be*, I thought.

But Miss Fritz didn't press for personal declarations.

She winked at me and welcomed Rachel to school once more.

"Whew, we did it," I told her as we headed to my lockers. "We're almost home free."

"Home free?" she muttered. "What's that?"

"I'll tell you later." I twirled my combination lock faster than most days. Now . . . if I could just keep Rachel from spilling the beans to the Alliteration Wizard, we'd be on our way. For the rest of the day.

"Mistress of Mirth!" I heard my alliterated nickname come floating down through the ocean of humanity in the hallway all the way to my locker.

"Jovial Jon," I said, turning around.

He stopped in his tracks, glancing at Rachel. "Friend or foe?"

"This is my *cousin* Rachel."

His face lit up. "Well, any relative of Merry's is a friend of mine," he said, pouring on the charm.

"Good to meetcha," she said.

I wondered how on earth Rachel had remembered to substitute the word *good* for *gut.* Thinking that I would just reach up and grab my books from my locker and get going, I caught myself. I absorbed the interesting fact that Jon seemed taken with the likes of my thoroughly modern Amish cousin, clearly not remembering her from our Christmas skating party.

He was still gazing at her as I explained. "Rachel's here visiting today. She's my guest."

They were in the middle of a proper handshake, and I waited for a moment till the initial greetings had been exchanged. Oddly enough, Jon seemed to have forgotten all about alliteration-eze and our before-the-first-bell word game frenzy.

Evidently, something more important was occupying the empty space in his brain.

Someone.

I watched, expecting him to back away from my locker, smile his biggest smile, and say "see ya around," but this non-Merry encounter was lasting longer than usual. Awkwardly so.

"Say, that was some science assignment," I said, choosing *s* to bait him.

He looked at me momentarily, almost dazed. "You're right."

No alliteration comeback? What was going on?

I tried again. "Where's the wonderful word Wizard?"

W—one of his favorite letters, I thought.

"I'll walk you to homeroom," he said, meaning both of us. But he didn't jump on the word game.

Truly amazing!

So we walked, the three of us. I couldn't begin to set him straight about who Rachel really was, not without blowing the whistle on her little charade. But it was all I could do to stifle a giggle as we moved through the crush of kids.

Wouldn't Jon be surprised to know that Rachel was Amish? Wouldn't he be embarrassed, too, that his alluring alliteration skills had just flown the coop?

The boy was smitten. For the first time in his life he was showing signs of truly liking a girl, and it had to be Rachel Zook. An Amish girl, of all things!

 FOURTEEN 

"You have to keep Rachel's secret *all* day," I told Chelsea outside homeroom—after Jon said good-bye to Rachel and a total of zero words to me.

"No problem," she said.

"I'm trusting you not to tell a soul," I whispered, hoping Rachel was gawking at the students running to beat the bell, not listening in on my conversation with Chelsea.

Staring at me with those sea-green eyes, Chelsea teased, "Is there an echo in here?"

"Sorry, it's just that I've stumbled onto something that might help us beat Jon at his own game." I had to keep my voice low. Rachel was inching closer, leaning against the classroom door a few feet behind us.

"You've gotta be kidding—like what?"

We put our heads together. "He's nuts about Rachel."

"No way."

"It's true." I went on to explain that he'd stopped alliterating around her. "I tried to get him going twice this morning. No response. Couldn't even get him interested."

Chelsea shifted her pile of books from one arm to the other. "How do you know he won't start again?"

"That's what I wanna check out," I said. "At lunch, let's see what happens."

"Great idea." She was grinning now. "I'll invite Jon to sit with us. We'll throw around some phrases . . . see if he plays along. Maybe he'll want to show off for her."

"It's genius!"

She nodded. "For once, Merry, you're right about that dumb thing you're always saying."

Genius? I thought. What a wondrous word.

❧ ❧

Rachel was curious about everything, it seemed. She thumbed through my three-ring binder, reading all my homework assignments before each class. She was also quite taken with some of the posters of rock stars plastered inside various lockers. Other things, too. Like tiny vanity mirrors and shelves for hair brushes and makeup supplies.

"A school locker's like a mini home away from home," I tried to explain. "A pit stop . . . to check your face. You know, to see how you look before rushing off to class."

"Pit stop," she mumbled, trying on the word for size, I suppose. "Tell me about home free?"

I was surprised she'd remembered to ask. I did my best to describe a baseball game, with all three bases loaded.

"Oh jah, Amish play baseball all the time," she said. "I know . . . you must be talkin' about stealing home?"

"Well, sorta, only it's a little different when you say

you're 'home free.' It really means that you're almost where you want to be. You've almost accomplished what you set out to do."

"Ach yes, Merry. I think I see what you mean." Then she giggled.

I wasn't sure if she caught the connection between the ball game and the phrase. But she was having a good time here at school. A good morning, at least.

It would be entertaining to see what happened at lunch—that is, if Jon joined us. I wanted to start thinking in terms of alliterating most everything. Warming up in my mind, so to speak.

Across the aisle, Chelsea was firing up her brain during algebra class. I was almost positive, because I saw her making a list of *w* words.

I wished that Lissa and Ashley knew about lunch with Jon. They needed the most work on speaking alliteration-eze off the top of their heads. Still, I hoped that maybe today could be a practice round . . . or better. Since Rachel would be eating at our table, maybe her presence would distract Jon. Again.

I set about writing sentences with similar consonant sounds, wondering quite suddenly what Levi, Rachel's brother, would think of all this alliterating madness.

Thinking about Levi, I decided to write a letter later today, after I returned Rachel safely home. It had been several weeks since I'd taken time to write. Besides, I owed my Mennonite friend a letter.

Switching mental gears from Jon to Levi had nothing

to do with Rachel coming to school today. Nothing to do with Jon's obvious interest in her, either.

Nope. I had plenty of friends. Besides, why *should* I put all my eggs in one fickle Klein basket?

FIFTEEN

Everything happened too fast.

Chelsea, Lissa, and Ashley had seated themselves on one side of the lunchroom table. Rachel and I sat on the other side.

I was trying to explain our word game to Rachel, who nodded and smiled, keeping her comments few and far between.

"You just use the same beginning sound of a word as many times in a row as you can. Sometimes, we've even put a twenty-second time limit on it . . . or less."

"Oh" was all she said.

We—Chelsea, Lissa, Ashley, and I—began warming up, getting ready to catch the Wizard off guard, when he waltzed over.

"Sorry so late," he said, carrying a lunch tray.

I didn't have to guess where he'd want to sit. Politely, he asked if Rachel would mind if he sat next to her. She blushed sweetly and scooted over, closer to me.

Jon took her response as a "yes" and proceeded to set down his tray.

Chelsea got things going. "Ever wonder what words

work with all *w*'s?" she asked, looking directly at Jon.

He turned to Rachel, ignoring the enticement from Chelsea. "She talks funny, doesn't she?"

Smiling, Rachel said nothing.

I spoke up. "I say we have a practice round of alliteration-eze. And while we're at it, why wait till next week for the championship?"

"Go for it," Chelsea cheered.

"And may the best woman win," offered Lissa. A little weak with only two *w*'s in a row, but she was trying.

As for Ashley, it appeared that she was more taken with trying to decide if Jon was falling for Rachel than attempting to alliterate sentences. Fine with me. From what I'd observed, Jon wasn't about to make a big verbal impression on any of us. Maybe it was because Rachel was keeping mum, following my orders. After all, how easy *was* it to converse with someone who remained silent?

Or perhaps Rachel's demure demeanor had locked up the Wizard's brain. (The silent woman appeal does it every time!)

Whatever it was about Rachel Zook, Jon couldn't—or wouldn't—attempt to alliterate. At least not today.

It was more than frustrating. It was exasperating, and Chelsea told him so. "Look, Jon, we've been preparing for this word game thing of yours. Are you gonna play or not?"

He shrugged, then paused, glancing down at his plate. For the longest time, he just stared at it. Then when I was sure he was going to cut loose with a yard-long sentence of silliness, he just shook his head. "I'm bored with it, I guess."

"Bored?" Ashley piped up. "How could anybody be bored?"

I clapped for her. "Three *b*'s in a row—even one inside the word. Not bad."

"Atta girl, Ashley," cheered Chelsea. But it was Jon we were bribing—tempting him to play.

The Wizard was caught up in his new interest, however. "Would you like some ice cream?" he asked Rachel.

"Thank you," she said simply. And he was up and out of his seat.

I shook my head. "A marvelous mind is such a sad thing to waste."

"Meaning?" Lissa asked, reaching for a straw.

"The Wizard went a-walking," Chelsea said, giggling.

"He's horribly hard to handle," I spouted off. "Has to have his handicap." I wanted to say he'd forfeited his chances at the championship, but it wasn't really up to me to decide these things.

When he returned with the ice cream, he asked Rachel about her Anabaptist beliefs. Probably because she was wearing her veiling.

I wondered if now was a good time to set him straight—reveal all—and say she was Amish. Surveying the situation, I noticed that Rachel was particularly enjoying the attention. It would be heartless of me to pull the plug on their budding friendship.

Still, I wondered how Matthew Yoder might feel if he could see the two of them together. I didn't have to guess, really. Watching Jon talk to Rachel with such animation—

was it admiration, too?—seeing her nod or gesture bashfully, without saying much of anything, I knew exactly how the young Amishman, Rachel's beau, would feel.

Truly horrible!

SIXTEEN

"I told Jonathan Klein the truth after school," Rachel said as we hurried upstairs to my bedroom.

"About being Amish?"

"Jah." She smiled broadly. "Honestly, it feels awful gut to talk normal again."

"To say what you're used to saying? The *way* you're used to saying it?"

"For sure and for certain," said Rachel.

We scurried into my bedroom, and I closed the door. The conversation was headed in a very secretive direction.

"How did Jon react when you told him?" I had to know.

"He said he wasn't all that surprised. That I had a soft-spoken way 'bout me. Somethin' he admires in a woman."

A *woman*? Give me a break!

"And he wanted to know if he could come see me sometime."

I was as silent as if the air had been punched out of

me. "Did you say he could?" I asked, reaching for a bed pillow and hugging it.

She shook her head. "I didn't know what to tell him, really. If Matthew gets wind of this . . ."

I was hesitant to ask. "Does Matthew love you, Rachel?"

"Jah, I think so." She paused for a moment, then went on. "He's talking marriage someday, but I'm not for sure 'bout my feelin's for him, ya see. He's gonna be baptized come next spring, and I . . . I . . . Well, I just don't know yet what I want."

"I think *I* know," I said softly.

We were quiet for a time. She, sitting across from me on my desk chair, still wearing my sweater and designer jeans, and I, crossing my legs under me as I sat on the bed. The silence became awkward, yet I did not burst out with any more questions.

Outside, the wind blew hard against the windows, and the crows in the field across the road called back and forth.

At last, Rachel spoke. "Today was the first I'd ever let myself look from the outside in—from outside my Plain world, all the way back to the way Mam and Dat raised me."

"I thought so," I whispered. "You just wanted to experience a taste of modern life. Right?"

She sighed a long, deep breath. "I've lived a life separated from the world all these years. I guess I just hafta see it for myself."

"How does Jon Klein fit into all this?" I ventured, half scared of what she might say.

Her face burst into a radiant smile. "To be honest with ya, Levi, my brother, got all this a-stirred up in me," she admitted. "I never woulda thought of such a thing as doin' what I did today. Goin' to public school and all. Or becoming friends with an English boy."

"Levi's leaving SummerHill has changed things for lots of people," I said.

"Jah, it has." Again she was still. She got up and went to stand in front of my dresser mirror, reached for the brush, and began to undo her hair, making it Plain again. "Ya know what, Merry? I'm awful glad Levi did it. It was just what I needed to get me thinkin' 'bout my own future."

"So you might decide to go modern, then?"

She turned suddenly. "What do ya think it would be like, Merry?"

"To leave your church and your family?" I couldn't even begin to comprehend what she was saying.

"No . . . to follow your heart like Joseph Lapp did."

So it was the wayward Joseph—his forbidden photograph—that was at the core of Rachel's restlessness.

"I don't know, really." I wondered what I could say to make things right for her. "Sometimes a girl has to follow her heart, as long as her desires line up with what God has planned."

"Oh, divine providence? Jah, I know what you're sayin'."

But I wasn't so sure she did. The strict Amish view of such things didn't always jive with basic Christian beliefs.

"Getting back to Jonathan," I said a bit hesitantly. "Does he know you're my neighbor?"

She nodded, smiling. "*Now* he does."

"So you must've told him everything."

"Jah, even about the pictures in the hayloft. He'd like to have one—when they're developed, that is."

I gasped. She'd fallen hard and fast. And now Jon Klein was going to be the recipient of my handiwork. Oh, what was this world coming to?

Totally stressed, I headed for my walk-in closet, where I kept snack food in several shoe boxes. Rachel's eyes widened when I offered her some raisins and other goodies.

"Denki," she said, taking some thin pretzel sticks.

"If you keep talking about your plans, I'm afraid I'll have to eat up my whole stash of munchies," I told her.

"Ach, how come?"

I explained that stress made me hungry. "Always has."

"Oh." She nibbled on the snacks. But it was the faraway look in her eyes that worried the socks off me.

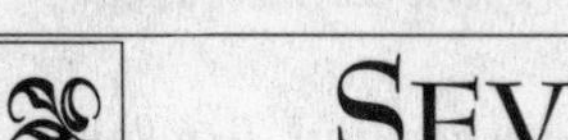

SEVENTEEN

Rachel talked me into letting her wear my best jeans home, under her Amish dress. I must've been out of my mind to let her, but she pleaded so desperately. How could I not grant her yet another wish?

After she left for home, I sat down with my best unlined stationery and penned a letter to Levi. Partway into it, I was struck with the notion that maybe he could help guide me through this thing with Rachel. Of course, I had to be cautious how I worded this section of the letter. I didn't want the boy rushing home from college to confront his sister.

Monday, February 23
Dear Levi,

Sorry it's been so long since I've written. Things are so hectic here, beginning with oodles of homework. Another thing: my dad's been sick this past week. His doctor ordered him to stay home, but he was so bored he tried to help me with my schoolwork nonstop. Can you believe it? Oh sure, he's smart enough and all, but having your fifty-year-old dad hover over your every math problem, well . . . it was difficult, to say the least.

I was wondering. What would you say to an Amish young person to encourage them in their beliefs? (That is, if the person seemed too eager to experience the outside world.)

Would you tell him or her to pray about it? To follow his or her heart? What?

I need your advice, Levi. I'm concerned for someone. Will you pray that I'll do the right thing?

Oh, I almost forgot. Last Saturday, I baby-sat for your little niece, Mary. What a doll! I'm delighted that your brother and sister-in-law were the ones who adopted her. I can see that God definitely had His hand in Mary's future.

I continued the letter, telling him about Chelsea's mother—how she was improving each day. And that Chelsea was attending church with me regularly. I even commented on the fact that a group of my girlfriends and I were hoping to defeat another classmate at a wacky word game.

It's called Alliteration-eze—an outlandish but lovely language. (See, I just wrote it!) You use the same consonants (or vowels) to begin words in a sentence. Here's another example: Levi listens to lectures at lunchtime.

Get it?

Well, it's about time for supper here. Hope you're doing all right at school. Everyone here in SummerHill misses you. So do I.

Your friend always,
Merry

I reread the letter, not even stumbling over the part

where I mentioned the word game. No second thoughts! Probably because I was growing up, maturing, I suppose. Why else would I want to blab the secret game to my former Amish boyfriend?

❧ ❧

After school the next day, I deposited my film at the local drugstore. It was only a couple of blocks from the school. I didn't have to worry about catching the bus today because Mom had planned to pick me up. We were going shopping. She—browsing at an antique store; me—searching for a new pair of school shoes.

The ones I'd been wearing were beginning to show signs of fatigue. Meaning, there was no passing them on to the Salvation Army. Not *this* pair! Too ratty.

Anyway, Mom met me in front of the drugstore, double-parking only briefly as I hurried to get in. "Where to?" she asked.

"Park City," I said. "*Somebody* oughta be having a sale on shoes, don't you think?"

She smiled, but I could tell she was preoccupied.

"Who's got a sale going on antiques?" I quizzed her.

That got her attention. "Alden's. I saw advertised in the paper a couple of highboys," she replied. "Let's synchronize our watches."

"Good idea."

"I'll be back in an hour or so, how's that?" she said.

"That's enough time for me; what about you?" I was trying not to laugh. In the not-so-distant past, Mom had been known to disappear, swallowed up by antique dealerships—Sometimes not resurfacing for a half day or more.

"Well, maybe if I set my watch so it beeps," she replied, grinning.

"Okay, then." She pulled into the mall parking lot. "Drop me off at Penney's. You can meet me there, too. In an hour and a half. Okay?"

She promised not to forget.

"See ya later," I called to her.

❧ ❧

Inside, I discovered a deserted mall. The corridors were vacant, and only a few people, mostly adults, were sprinkled here and there. It was Tuesday—one week after the popular Presidents' Day sales. Maybe the good stuff had already been purchased. I thought about that, wondering why I hadn't gone on the hunt for shoe sales *last* weekend.

Then I remembered. I'd had the Valentine's Day sleepover. Far more important than any shopping spree!

I removed my jacket, wishing I didn't have to lug it around—one of the worst things about wintertime shopping. You bundled up to go outside, but once indoors, a jacket, hat, scarf, and gloves were a nuisance.

Quickly, I headed for the Value Shoe Store, scanning the window displays. Surely this was the best place for something practical and affordable. I picked out three pairs, then bunched up my jacket and stuffed it under one of the tiny stools and began trying on shoes.

I was well into my second pair when I noticed another customer wander in. The teen girl had light brown hair and the bluest eyes. I wouldn't have given her a second look—mostly because she was so made up—but there was something about her. . . .

She seemed familiar. But why?

Another glance told me, and I nearly choked. Rachel Zook was here, looking downright hideous. Tight corduroy skirt, too short. Silk blouse, low cut. Hair in long, flowing waves about her shoulders. Actually, the hairstyle was the only good thing.

I ducked my head, hoping she wouldn't find me gawking, instead paying attention to the size and fit of the shoes I was trying on. At least, I pretended to.

"Merry? Is that you?" she called to me.

What should I say? I didn't quite know, but I turned around and looked up. "Hi," I said.

"What'sa matter with ya? You look like ya've just seen a ghost."

"A ghost wouldn't be so startling," I muttered. "How'd *you* get here?"

"Hitched a buggy ride with a friend and caught the bus." She looked around, pulling boxes of shoes down off the shelves, one after another. " 'Spose they've got red dancing slippers?" she asked.

"What do you want shoes like that for?" I asked.

"Oh, ya never know where you'll end up," she said in the sassiest voice.

"Rachel," I whispered to her, now standing up. "Are you nuts?"

She stepped back, shrugging my hands off her shoulders. "Listen here. I'm tired of doin' things the Old Way. This is *my* time, Merry. Do ya hear?"

I shook my head, fearing for her. "I'd hate to see you get hurt." Sighing, I continued. "Rachel, you can't go around dressed like that. It's not becoming to a lady."

She was laughing now, not the hearty, country laugh I was used to. It was a silly, fickle sort of giggling. Like she was purposely calling attention to herself. "What do ya think the 'running around' years are supposed to be for, anyhow?" she said, putting on some poppy-red high heels and wobbling around in them.

"Your mother would cry a river if she could see you," I replied. "And . . . she's not the only one."

Rachel stopped prancing around. "What do ya mean?"

"Levi, your brother. That's what I mean. Don't break his heart."

She squared her shoulders. "He broke mine. And Mam's and Dat's—all the People. What's good for the goose is good for the gander."

"Oh, Rachel. *Please*. You're not yourself. You're—"

"You said it, Merry! I'm *not* myself. I don't wanna be Rachel Zook anymore." And with that, she flounced off to pay for her new red shoes.

I wanted to run after her, keep her from buying the gawdy things—with all of my heart I wanted to. But something kept me locked up. Maybe it was fear. Was I too frightened to go after her? Afraid she'd push me away, not heed my words?

Shoving the boxes back onto the shelves, I was in no mood for trying on shoes. I'd just have to wear my old ones a few days longer.

There was only one thing to do. *Someone* could help

Rachel. I was almost sure of it. Not one-hundred-percent-amen sure as usual. But my idea was worth a try.

Avoiding Rachel at the cashier, I rushed past her, out of the store. I felt my heart thumping hard as I looked in both directions, from one end of the mall to the other.

Where, oh, where was the nearest telephone?

 EIGHTEEN 

"May I speak to Jonathan, please?" I said into the receiver.

"Certainly," his mother said. "How are you, Merry?"

I wasn't surprised that she recognized my voice. "Fine, thanks. And . . . I'm sorry to bother you, but this is sort of an emergency."

Jon came on the line quickly. "Merry, are you all right?"

"Well, I've been better." I began to fill him in on Rachel. "She's way out there somewhere in her head. First, she talked me into taking her picture. Then it was the school thing. And now this."

"Slow down," he said calmly. "How can I help?"

I was relieved. He was saying all the right things.

"Do you like Rachel? I mean, do you *care* anything about her?"

He was silent for a moment. "I liked what I saw the other day, yes. But I don't want to influence her away from her lifestyle."

"But if you could, would you persuade her to rethink where she seems to be headed?" I asked, wondering if he could hear the pleading in my heart.

The answer came softly. "What do you want me to do, Merry?" No alliteration-eze. None. He was playing straight with me.

"Here's my idea. Invite Rachel to go somewhere with you. For a soda or something. Tell her she should be herself. Forget about painting up and dressing like someone she's not."

"I think I could do that." He decided on a time—tomorrow after school. "If she agrees, let her know that I'll meet her at Pinocchio's. My treat."

I thanked him and hung up. My heart sank. This was one of the hardest things I'd ever done—setting up *my* guy with a girl gone goofy.

Keeping my eyes peeled, I searched the mall for Rachel. In every department store and dress shop, I looked. But she was nowhere to be found.

In my despair, I headed back to Penney's, attempting to ignore the ever-growing population of disheveled-looking teenagers on every corner. It wasn't until I'd passed several gift shops, a potpourri place, and the food court that I spotted my friend.

She was talking to a boy who was sporting a black leather jacket and boots, and I wasn't sure, but it looked like he had on black fingerless gloves.

I watched as she smiled up at him, her face not nearly as innocent now as it had been yesterday at school.

Silently, I began to pray. *Dear Lord Jesus, help me to help Rachel.*

Suddenly, a mighty surge of confidence rose up in me. I marched over there to my friend and tapped her on the shoulder. "We need to talk," I said.

She turned around, offering a pathetic little smile. "What are ya doin' here? Spoilin' my fun?"

"I have a message from Jon Klein—remember him?"

Her eyes brightened. "Really? What's he want?" she whispered, glancing back at the leathered one.

"I'll tell you if you come with me," I coaxed.

"Excuse me," she said to the guy behind her. And she walked toward Penney's with me.

"Jon wants to see *you*. Tomorrow." I told her where and when.

"A date? Are ya sure?"

"One-hundred-percent-amen sure!" Whew, was I ever glad I could finally say that. And mean it.

"Need a ride?" I asked, having mixed feelings about her coming home with us. Mom might react negatively upon seeing Rachel like this. On the other hand, I was willing to do most anything to get her out of this mall and those wretched clothes!

"Do ya mind?" she said. "I suppose it's 'bout time for milkin'."

I checked my watch. "Hey, you're right."

❧ ❧

All that evening, I thought about Rachel. Couldn't help reliving the astonished look on my mother's face when she saw Rachel dressed as a worldly English girl. Mom was smart, though. She said nothing, instead going off on a tangent about her incredible finds at the antique shop.

Dad was quiet at the table, not his usual self. Mom

initiated plenty of conversation, though. Mostly centered around Rachel Zook's "wicked getup."

I didn't blame her for being so upset. She needed to vent it, get her disgust out of her system. I must admit, seeing Rachel with her skirt hiked up past her knees, her cat eyes from too much eyeliner—the whole freaky package was enough to make any mother cringe.

"What's come over Rachel?" she asked after describing the afternoon's scene for Dad's benefit.

"Rachel's gone berserk, that's what." I couldn't think of a better way to relate it.

"Is she thinking of leaving the Amish, like Levi did?" Mom asked.

Now was my chance to mark the difference between Levi and his silly sister. "Levi's called to be a minister," I insisted.

Dad wiped his mouth with a napkin and looked at me without a reply.

"Rachel has other things on her mind. And it has nothing to do with seeking the Lord for her future, that's for sure."

Mom's brown eyes were serious. "What a shame."

"Not only that—she's confused," I blurted. "Rachel doesn't really know what she wants at all."

Dad sipped his herb tea, then said, "I've passed her on the road, riding with Matthew Yoder in his courting buggy a time or two."

I nodded. "That's probably the biggest hurt. At least for Matthew. *She's* all mixed up, but *he* loves her."

Mom leaned back in her chair. "Well, most likely your friend will come to her senses in good time."

"I hope so . . . before it's too late." I was thinking about Jon's offer to take her for a soda. Tomorrow! If he could straighten her out, I'd be ever grateful. But if he couldn't, I'd have to push Levi even harder for answers in my next letter. Maybe even tell him outright who was worrying me so.

Worse, I felt truly responsible for the whole mess. If I just hadn't given in to Rachel's first request—taking her picture in the haymow—maybe none of this would be happening.

NINETEEN

Chelsea was waiting for me at my locker on Wednesday morning. "What's with the Wizard?" she said.

"Jon?"

She nodded. "He's acting so-o weird."

"What else is new?"

"He's all dressed up, like he's going to church or something," she told me.

Then I knew. "Oh, that."

"What?"

"Hey," I laughed. "That's *my* line."

"So tell me. Why's he wearing a button-down shirt and nice jeans to school?"

"It's Rachel . . . they have a date this afternoon."

She grabbed her throat. "Tell me you're kidding!"

"Actually, I'm not. It was my idea."

She studied me, her eyes narrowing slowly. "You set it up? Are you crazy?"

"For a very good cause," I said. "Trust me."

"Whatever."

We walked to homeroom together, and as we did, I tried to make her understand the strange things going on with Rachel. "She's freaking out—like a bird let out of a cage for the first time."

"Hmm. I wonder what it would be like, feeling imprisoned like that."

"Well, I'm hoping Jon can help her somehow. At least, that's my plan."

She pushed me aside comically, primping in my teeny locker mirror. "Let's just hope he doesn't decide to join up with her People and become Amish." She stepped back, the biggest smile spreading across her face. "Hey! An Amish Alliteration Wizard—not bad."

I laughed, knowing without a shadow of a doubt *that* would never happen.

"Shh! Here he comes now," I said, darting into homeroom. Chelsea followed close behind, and I took great pleasure in scrutinizing Jon's attire.

Chelsea wasn't kidding. He was dressed up really nice. For a split second I felt envious, left out. Wished he'd taken such pains to impress *me*.

He waved and smiled. I did the same, reaching for my assignment notebook, thumbing through its pages. The thought that I had no one to blame but myself for the way I felt continued to haunt me all through homeroom and beyond.

By the end of the school day, I was literally a wreck. Not only that, Jon was absolutely not allowing himself to be sucked into any of my many attempts to get him to alliterate. He just wouldn't.

"Is it true? Are you really bored with it?" I asked after last-period class.

"Off and on, I guess."

"Well, I don't get it. Just when I—*we*—were about to take you on with the championship and all. How could you bail out on us like that?"

He shrugged, picked up his books, and walked with me to the door. "To be honest with you, Merry, it was more fun when the game was kind of a secret."

"Oh." I hadn't ever considered that *he* would think of such a thing. But I was pleasantly surprised. And thinking back on what he'd just said made my heart skip a beat. Maybe there was still hope for Jon and me.

Then I remembered the after-school tête-á-tête I'd arranged for him with Rachel. What was I thinking?

Sighing, I said good-bye and headed off to my locker.

I was clicking off the numbers on my combination lock when Chelsea came up behind me. "Doing anything this minute?" she asked.

"Going home, that's all. Got tons of homework."

"I have an idea," she said, pushing her thick auburn locks behind one ear. "Since my mom's coming to pick me up, why don't you ride home with me."

"And?"

"We can do a little spying while we wait," she said.

Genius! I saw right through her. "Good idea. Why didn't *I* think of this?" We were off to Pinocchio's, the cozy little corner cafe down the street. "Hey, do you mind if I run and pick up my pictures first?"

A big grin stretched across her face. "Do I get a sneak preview?"

"All depends," I said.

"On what?"

"If the pictures turn out."

She snorted. "You mean there's a chance that the incredible photographer Merry Hanson could flub up a photo?"

I laughed with her, rushing into the drugstore.

❦ ❦

As it turned out, the pictures were pretty good. Most of them. Chelsea flipped through the stack as we situated ourselves at a table in the far end of Pinocchio's. How we ever got inside without being noticed by either Jon or Rachel, I don't know. But we'd been very discreet, keeping our faces turned the other way. Stuff like that.

Now that I sat here snooping on my friends, I wasn't so sure we should've come. And I told Chelsea so.

"Aw, Merry, don't be a spoil sport," she scolded. "You're enjoying this as much as I am."

I had to admit, part of me was. Except when Jon leaned across the table and covered Rachel's hand with his own. Oh, and the lovely smile that burst across her face in response to it!

This wasn't in the plan. Jon was supposed to encourage Rachel to be herself. Follow the road of obedience to parents and God, not make her fall in love with him, for Pete's sake!

But it was too late. Romantic things were happening, and I knew it by the way she never took her innocent eyes off him. Soon, she was taking out a pen from the pocket of *my* designer jeans and wrote something—probably her address—on a piece of paper.

I groaned repeatedly. Chelsea, who checked her watch for the tenth time, decided it was time to split. "We oughta be outside when my mom drives by," she said.

Reluctantly, I agreed, sliding out of the booth before the waitress ever got around to taking our orders. "Whatever we do, we can't let Jon and Rachel see us," I warned Chelsea.

Miraculously, we were able to slip away through a back exit. Home free!

❦ ❦

Hours later, Rachel stopped by to see me. I suppose it was timely, too, because I had lots of pictures to show her.

I was in the middle of a math haze, deep in homework when Mom called upstairs.

"Send her up." I closed my book, wondering what Rachel wanted with me after having spent the afternoon with Jon. Was she going to fill me in on every detail? I curled my toes beneath my socks, hoping not.

"Hullo, Cousin Merry," she said, breezing into my room.

"Wanna see some pictures?" I asked, pulling them out of the envelope.

Eyes bright, she sat on my bed, examining each shot, holding them as though they were priceless. Guess I might've felt the same way if I'd never seen myself in a photograph.

"Which one do you like best?" I asked.

She held up one of the pictures. The one where her hair was free. Without the veiling.

"I should've known you'd pick that one," I said, chuckling.

"This was hilarity, highly hidden. Jah?"

"You like your hair down best?" I asked, wondering why she was talking so weird.

She nodded. "Hanging hair is happy hair."

It hit me. "Did Jonathan teach you something today? A different way to talk?"

She absolutely beamed. "I wrote out words that started with *my* name . . . and his!"

Just great, I thought, frustrated. They'd spent their time playing the word game. And Jon had said he was bored with it. What a line!

She took out a billfold and paid me for the pictures. "Can you give this picture to Jonathan tomorrow?" she asked, still studying the hayloft setting. "He says he's anxious to get it."

I'll bet he is, I surmised. But I didn't say anything.

Here I'd thought getting Jon and Rachel together was the brightest thing I'd ever done. Wrong!

Still, I was stuck. "Sure, I'll give him the picture," I said. Then I got up the nerve to ask, "Did Jon say anything about your outfit, your makeup, or your styled hair?"

She glanced down at her skirt. "Ach, not really. But he *did* say something kinda interesting."

"What?"

"He said I should think about going out with him on a real date. If my parents wouldn't mind." Her eyes sparkled as she began to recount the afternoon.

Meanwhile, I was feeling rather limp inside. My plan to "save" Rachel from worldly English influences had completely backfired.

What would Levi think if he knew? I wouldn't be the one to inform him, that was for sure. And Chelsea? She'd be laughing in her soup. She wouldn't think it was so funny if she knew how I used to feel about the Alliteration Wizard.

He'd taught Rachel the word game just minutes after telling me he was bored with it. How could he lie to me that way?

Who could I turn to? And why did life have to be so complicated?

TWENTY

Rachel was right. Jon was thrilled to get her picture the next day. His face lit up like a neon sign as I handed it to him.

Hurt and a little more than mad, I turned to head for my locker.

"Whoa, Merry, wait up," he called after me.

Stunned once again that he hadn't used one of his favorite alliterated nicknames for me—*Mistress Merry* or *Merry, Mistress of Mirth*—I froze in place.

"Merry?"

Slowly, I turned around.

"Merry, what's wrong?"

I glanced down at the picture of my Amish girlfriend in his hand. Swallowing the anger away, I put on a smile. "Have fun alliterating—Amish style," I said.

"So . . . you heard?" He looked quite sheepish, as if he'd been caught with his hand in a cookie jar.

"Maybe you're just what Rachel needs to get her through this time in her life." I stared him down—literally. "Well, gotta run."

And I did. Scrambled right through the crowd of students and found a safe haven at my locker.

❧ ❧

Right after school, Nancy and Ella Mae Zook, Rachel's younger sisters, showed up at my back door. They had on matching green dresses and black pinafore-style aprons under their long black woolen shawls. "Do ya have a minute?" Nancy, the fourteen-year-old, asked.

"Come in." I led them into the kitchen.

Ella Mae, almost ten, whispered, "Can we go some place more private?"

Now I was worried. "Is this about Rachel?"

They nodded simultaneously.

Without further comment, I motioned them into the small sitting room off the kitchen. Closing the door behind me, I offered them a seat. I stood, however, bracing myself for what was to come.

Nancy blushed bright red. "We ain't here to point blame at ya, Merry, but, well . . ." She paused, adjusting her shawl.

Ella Mae continued. "Didja give Rachel them modern clothes to wear?"

I shouldn't have been surprised that they suspected me. "I loaned her a pair of jeans and a sweater last Monday, but I don't know where she got that short skirt . . . or that low-cut blouse." I shook my head, staring at the ceiling. "I don't even own clothes like that. Honest."

"Okay, then," Nancy said. "We believe ya."

I took a deep breath, wondering what more they had to ask. Hopefully, neither of them knew about the photo shoot in the hayloft. Or the forbidden visit to my high school.

"Our parents will be comin' home tomorrow," Nancy volunteered. "Rachel oughtn't to be struttin' around in such an awful getup."

I nodded. "Oh, I'm sure she'll put her Amish dress back on. She wouldn't want to show disrespect to your parents."

"Well, I don't know already," Ella Mae said. "She's been terrible haughty the last couple-a days."

"Jah, I can't figure what's come over her," Nancy replied.

I walked to the window, glancing out, then turned to face the girls. "You've heard of Rumschpringa, right?"

Nancy's face pinched up. "But, Merry, it don't hafta be this way. Not all of us sow wild oats."

"That's true." I knew lots of Plain young people who held devotedly to their upbringing. "But . . . does Rachel have a strong faith?"

Ella Mae looked puzzled. "In God?"

"Why, sure she does," Nancy said. "We *all* do. It's part of bein' Amish."

Her answer left me hanging. Sounded to me like Nancy just assumed that if you were Amish you were automatically a Christian. "Well, I'm sorry you have to go through this with Rachel. She just seems sorta mixed up, I guess."

"Jah, ferhoodled," Ella Mae muttered.

"You can say that again," Nancy agreed.

I didn't tell them their sister was so out of it that she'd linked up with one of my favorite guy friends. That she was willing to entertain him by spouting off alliterated phrases, sneaking out of the house to meet him at corner cafes. Nope. I didn't blurt any of that.

Thinking they were about ready to head back home, I invited them to have a cup of hot cocoa.

"Denki," they said, staying seated.

Awkwardly, I shuffled my feet and twiddled my thumbs.

Then Nancy, who looked rather glum, spoke up. "To top it off, Matthew Yoder stopped by today," she said. "Such a right nice and thoughtful boy, he is."

"Jah." Ella Mae was shaking her head.

I listened, wondering why these girls thought so much of their big sister's boyfriend.

"He came over in his new open buggy," Nancy whispered.

"Jah, it's unheard of. No fella in his right mind wants to be seen callin' on a girl in broad daylight. Courtin's done in secret—at night."

I chimed in. "I've heard that, too."

"But Matthew came right up to the front door," Nancy explained. " 'Course, Rachel wasn't home."

Because she was having sodas with Jon Klein, I thought.

"What do you think Matthew wanted?" I asked naively.

"Rachel . . . he wanted to see Rachel. We told him she was off to town." Ella Mae was grinning now, her fingers running along the loose strings of her kapp.

"Did he come to ask her for a date . . . or whatever?" I said, fumbling over the correct Amish word.

"Ach, he seemed upset—wanted to know why she was

actin' so peculiar lately," Nancy said. "Probably wanted to drive her to the next Singin' in his new buggy. Jah, that's what he wanted with her."

"But I thought the girl's brother is supposed to take her to the Singing. What about that?" I asked.

"The big brothers usually do, but Curly John's married now, so I guess Matthew don't wanna wait around for young Aaron to grow up." Nancy looked sharply at me, and a peculiar expression crossed her face. " 'Course, if Levi were home here where he belongs, *he* could be takin' Rachel . . . and lettin' Matthew drive her home. That's the way it's s'posed to be done."

I shivered a bit. Felt as if they were blaming *me* for Levi not living at home anymore—helping his father farm the land, helping his sister snag a husband. . . .

"It was never my idea for Levi to go away to college," I said softly.

"No . . . no. It's nobody's fault, really." Nancy looked more sad than mad. "Guess we'd best be leavin' now."

The conversation had gone in circles. Nothing had been solved. As far as they were concerned, Rachel had only one night to get her act together. To prepare her clothing and her attitude for her parents' return.

What could I do to talk sense into her?

I struggled with that question long after Rachel's sisters left. If I could just share everything with my parents. They'd know what to do, maybe. But I'd promised Rachel and felt I couldn't go back on my word.

Finally, with my head spinning with ideas and more worries than could fill an apple barrel, I put on my jacket and headed outdoors.

Fortunately, Mom was in her sewing room making phone calls to several antique dealers. I found that out when I told her I was going for a walk. She pointed to her long list, smiled, and waved me on.

I must say that I was glad she hadn't happened in on my not-so-friendly discussion with our Amish neighbors just now. *That* was definitely something to be thankful for.

❧ ❧

Outside, the air was frosty and sweet. I kept my mouth closed and breathed through my nose so my lungs wouldn't freeze up. That's how cold it was.

Deciding to walk up the hill toward Chelsea's house, I hummed a Sunday school song. I thought of Jon and how he'd hurt me. Again. When would I ever learn my lesson?

Switching to someone more dependable, I thought of Levi. I could hardly wait for him to write back. He should've gotten my letter by now, I guessed. And surely he'd have some advice for me. Because I was desperate.

Just then, up ahead, I saw a horse and buggy coming toward me. The horse's hooves against the snow-packed road sounded more like muffled thuds than the *clippity-clops* of summer.

I prepared to wave at whichever Amish neighbor might be coming. What a surprise to see that Matthew Yoder was the driver. And the girl? The girl was definitely *not* Rachel Zook!

Trying to be polite, I smiled, refusing to stare at Rachel's competition. "Hi, Matthew!" I called, waving.

"Hullo, Merry. How are ya?" His voice floated off, out to the cornfield as the carriage passed me.

"Just look what you've gone and done, Rachel," I whispered to myself.

Instantly, I knew why Matthew Yoder was out parading his "date" on SummerHill Lane in broad daylight.

Spinning around, I slid back down the hill. Maybe there was still time to help Rachel with the afternoon milking. Hopefully, there was still time to help her get her head on straight. Finally!

TWENTY-ONE

I ran all the way through the snow, even taking the shortcut through the willow grove. Rachel looked surprised to see me as I dashed breathlessly into the barn.

The smell of hay was sweet in my nose, but my heart trembled with what I had to do. "Rachel, I have to talk to you."

She stopped wiping down the cow's udder and stood tall, staring at me. "What is it, Merry?"

"I hate to be a bearer of bad tidings, but I think you should know something."

"Jah?"

"It's about your Amish boyfriend." I told her everything—about Matthew and his new buggy and his new girl.

Rachel took the news mighty hard at first. Tears sprang up in her eyes. She turned and tried to conceal them, but I saw them just the same.

She wiped her face on the back of her sleeve, and we talked some more. After rethinking the situation with Matthew and herself out loud, she was more positive.

"Maybe he *was* just tryin' to get my attention. And that other girl—wish I knew who she was."

We started to laugh about it. "Jealousy is a cruel taskmaster," I said, speaking for myself.

She nodded in agreement. "Guess I oughta be thankin' ya, Merry. I'm glad ya told me." Her face was serious and drawn now. "I best be changin' out of these jeans of yours," she was quick to say.

I didn't go inside with her when she invited me but said my good-byes out by the milk house. "Hope it's not too late for you and Matthew," I called back.

She shook her head. "Don'tcha worry none."

Running toward the main road, I felt that I'd done the right thing for Rachel—at last! Of course, telling her about Matthew wasn't only going to benefit *her*. Matthew, if he hadn't truly linked up with someone new, might be real glad to take his old girlfriend back. That is, if she decided to forget about her "running around" nonsense and embrace the Old Ways once again. And if Matthew loved her as much as she thought he did.

❧ ❧

After supper, Levi called. "I got your letter, Merry."

I was startled for a moment. "Uh . . . it's nice to hear your voice, Levi, but I didn't expect you to call me." Now I felt funny having written for his advice.

"It's not a problem. Honest, it isn't."

His "ain't" is missing, I thought. The sign of a truly educated man.

"How's everything at school?" I asked.

"I'm always busy with studies, but the Lord is good. I'm learning to trust Him daily."

I couldn't get over how different he sounded. And in

only a few short months. "I'm glad you're happy there." I really didn't know what else to say.

"About your letter, Merry—I'd be lying to you if I didn't say that I suspect the person in your letter is my sister."

Surprised at his words, I just listened.

"Rachel's impulsive now, that's all . . . doesn't quite know where she's headed."

"You're probably right, but she'd never forgive me if she knew I told you," I admitted.

He breathed softly into the phone. Then, "My best advice to you is to pray for Rachel."

"Does she ever read the Bible?" I asked, knowing that most Amish read only the Old Testament.

"Now that I'm not home, I couldn't say."

I went on to tell him about her visit to my school. And her interest in modern clothes. "I wish she'd settle down a bit," I said. "I can't get used to *this* Rachel."

He laughed softly. "And to think that you had to go through all this—on some level—with me last summer, Merry."

"Oh, it wasn't so bad."

"My searching brought me to the Lord Jesus. I'm ever so thankful." Then he asked about my dad. "Is he feeling better?"

"Dad's doing fine now, but he's been talking about an early retirement. So I don't know what he's thinking."

"Really? Maybe he'll have time to travel more. He's always wanted to go on at least two mission trips a year," he said.

I grinned. "He told *you* about that?"

"Missionary work is a topic dear to both your dad's and my heart," he remarked.

"Just tonight at the table, Dad suggested that I come with him and Mom on a trip to Costa Rica over spring break."

"Do it!" Levi exclaimed. "You won't be sorry."

"Dad thinks I'd be a good photojournalist for the church."

"I hadn't thought of that, but he's right." His voice grew softer. "Maybe *that's* where your 'call' lies, Merry."

I'd never thought of my "call" from the Lord coming in the form of something I loved to do as a hobby. But now that Levi mentioned it, it made good sense.

"I'll think about it," I told him.

"Good, then. We'll talk soon, I hope."

"Thanks for calling, Levi."

"I miss you, Merry."

My heart nearly stopped. And I knew I missed him, too. More than ever.

"Oh, about talking in alliterated sentences," he added. "I've tried a few myself. I'll e-mail them to you."

"Great. I'll look forward to that."

We said good-bye and hung up.

❦ ❦

As promised, I received his e-mail.

Hi, Merry,

Here's my alliteration for the day: Hope for happiness, holiness, humility, and honor—no halfhearted, ho-hum hypocrisy.

—Levi

❧ ❧

I had to call Chelsea. "You'll never guess who's the new Alliteration Wizard!"

"I give up."

"No . . . you have to guess," I insisted.

"C'mon, Merry, I don't have time for games."

"Oh, so you're not playing, either?" I taunted.

"Who's not?" she asked.

"Well, not so long ago Jon wasn't. Or at least he said he wasn't."

"That's strange."

"What?"

"He just called here and was babbling baloney," she said.

I laughed. "So the former Wizard's making a comeback!"

"And maybe *you've* got him back?" she asked.

"Oh," I sighed. "I'm not so sure about Jon anymore." I felt the pain anew.

"Oh really?" She was probing for more details, but I had to put her off. Besides, Levi was on my mind. I was dying to tell her how excited I was about *his* call. "Levi Zook's an incredible alliterater."

"How do you know?"

I told her about the e-mail—the many, many *h*'s in a row. "He's truly amazing."

"With words or just in general?" she asked, laughing.

I wasn't ready to divulge any more secrets. Not just yet. But I did tell her about my timely encounter with Matthew Yoder on SummerHill Lane. "Rachel's through with running around," I said. "I'm one-hundred-percent-amen sure!"

"If you say so," she replied.

We giggled briefly, then hung up.

❦ ❦

Mom wanted to know what was so funny. "Glad you're having such a good week," she commented.

"Well, none of my cats got run over," I said, heading for the stairs and a mountain of homework. "And my pictures all turned out to be truly wonderful."

"Honey, you're not making much sense," she pointed out.

"You're right." I rushed to my room before she could call any more comments up to me.

I plopped on my bed, gathered my furry foursome around me, and thought of Joseph Lapp. "Well, I guess we have him to thank for the total chaos this week," I told them. "I think Rachel and her brother must share some of his genes."

Abednego eyeballed me as if to say, *Look who's talking.*

"Hey, I've been on both sides of the fence—the inside *and* the outside—and you know what?"

He meowed politely.

"It's not so much where you are; it's who you know. And I'm not talking riddles here, boys." I bowed my head. It was time for a personal chat with my heavenly Father—about Rachel and her future, about Levi and his, and about my own uncertainties. About life in general.

TWENTY-TWO

Weeks later Dad decided, after all was said and done, that he would take early retirement from the hospital. And he and Mom are planning an overseas trip. I'm invited but can't miss that much school. So Miss Spindler—Old Hawk Eyes, the neighbor lady behind us—has agreed to let me stay with her.

Maybe now I'll have a chance to do some sleuthing over there. I've been dying to know how she keeps such a close eye on everybody in SummerHill.

As for my baby-sitting job, it's earning me some spending money. The best part is getting to see sweet little Mary every weekend.

Levi's coming home for spring break, and it's for sure! I found out yesterday from Rachel, who, by the way, is behaving like her old self once again. In fact, I can hardly remember what she looked like in a short skirt and curled hair.

She's wearing her veiled covering consistently—*reverently*—and seems more content with being Plain. "I'm where I belonged all along," she told me recently.

Matthew Yoder forgave her in an instant. Last I heard,

they're taking baptismal classes together come spring. I wouldn't be surprised if there's another wedding coming up in a year or so.

Now, if I can just get my designer jeans back from her sometime. Souvenirs of wayward days probably aren't the best thing to keep around. I've told Rachel that, but she just smiles and says, "Looking at them every so often and Joseph Lapp's secret picture, too, are what help keep me Amish."

I don't ask "What?" and play dumb like I often do. I listen sincerely with my heart and pray . . . and try to understand. That's the best a friend can do, with or without the moon.

From Beverly . . . To You

I'm delighted that you're reading SUMMERHILL SECRETS. Merry Hanson is such a fascinating character—I can't begin to count the times I laughed while writing her humorous scenes. And I must admit, I always cry with her.

Not so long ago, I was Merry's age, growing up in Lancaster County, the home of the Pennsylvania Dutch—my birthplace. My grandma Buchwalter was Mennonite, as were many of my mother's aunts, uncles, and cousins. Some of my school friends were also Mennonite, so my interest and appreciation for the "plain" folk began early.

It is they, the Mennonite and Amish people—farmers, carpenters, blacksmiths, shopkeepers, quiltmakers, teachers, schoolchildren, and bed and breakfast owners—who best assisted me with the research for this series. Even though I have kept their identity private, I am thankful for these wonderfully honest and helpful friends.

If you want to learn more about Rachel Zook and her people, ask for my Amish bibliography when you write. I'll send you the book list along with my latest newsletter. Please include a *self-addressed, stamped envelope* for all correspondence. Thanks!

Beverly Lewis
℅Bethany House Publishers
11400 Hampshire Ave. S.
Minneapolis, MN 55438